G000138178

A Collector's Piece

From the pen of:

www.ncmpublishing.com

A Cold Piece
Written by: Ni'cola Mitchell
Edited by: David Goode
Text Formation: Write On Promotions
Cover Design and Layout: Rickey Maye
Printed in the United States of America

Dedication

To everyone that God has placed into my life for a reason. The ones, that have laughed with me, cried with me, prayed with me, and for the most part listens to with an open heart. I love all of you. I would not be here without any of you.

To Courtenay thank you for showing me that no matters what happens in life, you pray about it and get back up again. Your strength and wisdom has really kept me going when times are truly hard.

To Mama Cookie. You are one of the strongest women that I know. During the process of me writing this book, you have been here to guide me even when you were the one that required the attention. I love you ma am, and thank you for being the BEST mother that you could be.

Ni'cola

Acknowledgements

To my parents. **Mommy**, I am honestly impressed by the friendship that has developed. You went from being my Mom, to one of my good friends. Thank you and I love you.

Daddy. Daddy. Daddy. LOL. Even though you have such a strange sarcastic sense of humor, (that only the two of us know that is really out of love,) you are my superhero and I thank you. When I need you the most you are always here and I love you for that.

To my girls **Destani Imani**. It is wonderful seeing the beautiful young woman that you have grown into. Mini me… I tear up every time I think about you.

Diamond Lynn. You have metamorphosed into this mature teenager that is bright, intelligent and funny. The two of you are the wind beneath my wings. You push me, mold me, and most of all just give me and unconditional love for being your Mommy. I love you ladies!

To My Sisters. Especially **Sheila, Debbie, and NeNe.** You ladies are so protective of me and I thank you. Whenever I needed you, no matter what it is was for, especially while I was writing this emotional piece, you are always there. I love you and I thank you. For the longest time, I didn't think that life was worth living since Janet has passed, but I can honestly say between the three of you, you have made it bittersweet.

*To Ms. **Sharda Smith***. Girl I am so proud of you in more ways than one. You have matured so much and sometimes, I feel as if you are the aunt.. LOL. Thank you for your constant push. I love you little Nicki....

*To Ms. **Tamika Newhouse***... Girlllll all I can say is this. Thank you for being my rock. There is no way else to describe you. I love you.

*To Ms. **Kolanda Scott***. Thank you for being more than just a publicist. You are one of the best friends that I have. Love you boo.

*To Mr. **Reggie Joyce***. Thank you for stepping in and uplifting my career. You Rock.

*To Mr. **Chris Hicks***. Man I love you! You are more than a literary brother to me. I respect your business sense, your professionalism, and your high regards for me...

*To Mr. **Q.B. Wells*** You are an amazing friend/confidant. Your constant words of encouragement uplifts me. I love you my dude. ☺

To the rest of my family, especially my cousins, **Holly, Nyeisha, Blossom, Trish, and Taysia**. Ladies you are the Bomb.com. You have held me down in more ways than one, and I love you for it. To the rest of you my **Mitchell, Smith, Lefear, Ballentine, and Taylor** family members. I wouldn't be here without you, Trust and believe that.

To my literary Sistah's: **Rekaya Gibson**. Girl. I can honestly say that you give me balance. You were one of the first to believe in me and I love and thank you for it.

Queen BG Girl Boom! LOL. You came into my life, and basically told me you were not going anywhere. I love you.

Loretta Walls. Hey boo. Do you remember that first day that I contacted you asking you for advice? Are you getting tired me yet because I am still asking. LOL. Girl I love you. I am #TeamNuCherte

Toshia Shaw, I mean Ms. Tosh Lac. Can I be like you when I grow up! LOL. God places people in your life for a reason. After meeting you, I am def. a believer on that one. I love you.

To my friends/extended family. Especially **Andrice, Alisa, TJ, Quinn, Raenelda, Monica, Nicola, Steevie, CJ, Jermial, Richard, and Tina**, I don't know how I can repay you for that constant love that you all give me. Thank you.

To the rest of my literary family, **Omar Tyree, Corey Barnes, Sistar Tea, Dawn Michelle, Eyone Williams, Norris Pimpton, Moses Miller, David Good, Joey Pinkney, Faydra Dunn, Michael McGrew, Kwan, JM Benjamin, Andrionna Williams, Eric Deloach, Allyson Deese, and Elissa Gabrielle**. Thank you for the constant support, information, and love. I wouldn't be here without you.

To the ladies of NCM Publishing. **Rekaya, Imani, Dreama, Patricia, Faatima, Cynthia, Tamika, Danisha, Shawna, Souraya, and Alisa**.

Thank you for trusting and believing that I can bring your projects to life. You guys are more than just authors, you are my family, and I love you all! 2012 is going to be a great year! #TeamNCMPublishing.

I want to say thank you to all of the readers that has been following me since Over and Over Again, the book clubs that has hosted and welcomed me, and to all of the bookstores that has housed my books and the works of NCM Publishing, especially Barnes and Nobles on Rainbow and Lake Mead in Vegas. Thank you Crystal and Terry for so much love and support.

If there is anyone else that I have missed, I am so sorry; you know I have ADHD... Lol. I will get you next time around.

The best is yet to come......

Mental (men tl)

Adj.

1. Of or relating to the mind; intellectual: *mental powers.*
2. Executed or performed by the mind; existing in the mind: *mental images of happy times.*
3. Of, relating to, or affected by a disorder of the mind.

Instability (in sta bil I ty)

Noun

1. Lack of physical stability: unsteadiness
2. The quality or condition of being erratic or undependable: *emotional instability; political instability*

Together = A Cold Piece

A Cold Piece

Table of Contents

LET ME WORK ON THAT

NEVER PREPARED

UNFORTUNATE CIRCUMSTANCES

SOMEBODY PRAYED FOR ME

GET THE AUTHORITIES INVOLVED

TAKING LOSSES

FINALLY THE TRUTH

PEANUTS

BACK DOWN MEMORY LANE

ENOUGH IS ENOUGH

A COLD PIECE

Prologue

"Gabrielle!" I screamed kicking the door. I could hear her screaming for her life from inside, and there was nothing that I could do about it. My left arm was limp and bloody, and you could still see the smoke coming from the hole that the bullet created.

I prayed under my breath, "Dear Lord, please help her. Please let me save her," as I continued to kick the door. Lisa was at the end of her rope, and there was no point of return. She believed that her life was over, and there was only one person to blame, and that was Gabrielle.

My body was weak, and my vision was getting blurry, but I could not give up. Gabrielle was in danger, and I was the cause. That was the worse feeling in the world.

Another gunshot blast rung out, Gabrielle yelled out again.

Where the hell is the police, I thought to myself; feeling helpless and insecure. Taking in a deep breath, I attempted to regain my composure as I kicked the door hopefully for the last time.

Boom! Another gunshot rang out. This time it was not followed by a cry.

Changes

Lisa

"Right there baby, mmmmm right there!" Anthony moaned as I thrust my hips down on his pelvis again and again. It was five o'clock in the morning, and just like that new song that T-Pain was singing on the radio, *conversations got boring....* and I mean literally got boring.

I woke up my husband at four forty-five, so that we can have some pillow talk before he had to get ready for work, as I do every morning. I started the conversation telling him that I was thinking about having lunch with him today, and that is when things went to the left.

Anthony leaned in and kissed me, I melted like butter. His kiss was so slow, soft, and passionate that it didn't matter that we both had morning breath. Whispering my name occasionally between kisses, I felt my body begin to tremble.

Thirteen minutes later, I was now bottomless and straddled across his lap, bouncing up and down, gyrating back and forth as if my life depended on it. I had a vice grip lock on his shoulders as I used him for balance and support. Even though Anthony and I have been married for six years, I still had to hold on tight and take in deep breaths every time we had sex. My husband was well endowed, and my body is still trying to get used to it.

"I AM GOING TO CUM, LISA GET UP!" He yelled as he thrust his hips into my body one last time guiding me off of him. Quickly, I hopped up watching Anthony guide the seeds of his children into the towel that we always kept next to the bed.

2

A Cold Piece

"Babe, can you turn the shower on for me?" Anthony asked as he got up and headed towards the closet.

He can't be serious right now, I thought to myself stretching my arms up over my head. He made me put it on him like that, and now wants me to start the shower?

"Okay baby, give me one second. I need to catch my wind. Someone wore me out this morning, and I am realizing that I am really an old lady." I said through a big smile.

My husband is so damn sexy, I thought to myself admiring the firmness of his backside which got me all horny again. Carrying his favorite Armani suit, and tan colored gators, Anthony went into the bathroom and started the shower himself.

"Don't worry, I got it. I know your age is starting to get to you, and you can't hang anymore," he replied while chuckling.

Anthony is two years younger than me, but one would never know it. He had the finesse and sophistication of a man twice his age. When one of the major book store chains went out of business several years ago, Anthony went ahead and purchased as many as he could.

I thought it was a bad idea because the world was coming into the e-book phase, but when my husband has his mind made up, there is no stopping him.

Anthony comes from what is known as "Old Money," and has never wanted for anything. He graduated from Massachusetts Institute of Technology, where he majored in business. Between his exclusive college education, and the hands on education from his family lineage of businessmen, Anthony has always come out on top with his business ventures.

After only a year and a half, not only did Anthony have the struggling store chain back up and running, but we were now the worldwide leader in the e-book market.

I had to admit, my baby was the complete package: sex appeal, brains and an abundance of patience that can make you go crazy. Anthony was the type of person that played chess with you at all times, and you didn't even know it.

I heard the water pressure change, which meant that Anthony was in the shower. I waited a few more moments, and quietly rolled over to his side of the bed. I waited a few *more* moments before I grabbed his phone off of the nightstand.

Hmmm.... Three text messages. I wondered to myself. I know that Anthony loved me, but one could never be too trusting.

Ever since I met Anthony, I was always competing with beautiful women. I know a lot of people may think that I have it in the bag since I am technically supposed to be his *trophy wife*, but being married to a 6 foot

5, caramel skinned, articulate black man gave me a run for my money.

You see, I didn't come from money. To some people, before I met Anthony, I may even have been considered white trash, but Anthony never made me feel like that.

While Anthony was studying at MIT, I was dancing at a strip club not too far from the condominium that he lived in. I had only started dancing at the club two weeks prior to meeting him because I was in a dilemma. I was eight weeks pregnant and needed abortion money. Anthony frequented the club often, and knew that I was new.

Anthony sat alone in the corner drinking Stella beers but I felt his eyes on me as soon as he stepped in the room. I told myself that I wouldn't mess with another black man, since the guy that knocked me up, was a black athlete, that literary hit it, then split the scene.

A Cold Piece

Anthony paid for a private dance, but surprised me when he took me to the back. The only thing that he wanted to do was talk, which also shocked the hell out of me.

After about thirty minutes of straight conversation, he asked me how much he would have to pay so that I can leave with him.

"I am not a prostitute!" I exclaimed quickly getting up. I was lost in translation admiring the strength in his jaw as he spoke. My mind was flashing warning signs, but the sensation between my legs was telling me what the hell.

I knew that I wanted to sleep with this man, but in a normal situation, I would never leave with anyone. Even though I was desperate for money, I still had my standards.

"Baby girl, I didn't mean it like that," Anthony reassured me, grabbing my hand. "Deep in my heart, I feel as if you don't belong here, and wanted to chill with you outside of the club. I just want to get to know you better, that's all." Anthony finished while flashing me a heart melting smile.

I wanted this brother so badly and didn't know how to take it. I finally agreed and we have been inseparable ever since.

Being with Anthony came with the price of all types of beautiful women throwing themselves at him all the time. After everything that I have been through in my past, I was not going to lose my knight in shining armor to some random chick on the street.

This is why I constantly went through his phone. I needed the reassurance that everything was okay at all times. I knew the old saying that if you go looking for trouble, it's going to knock on your door; but I just had to take that chance when it came to my marriage.

I opened the text message screen on his phone, and my heart sank.

8

A Cold Piece

Wake up.

The message read from his new young Spanish assistant Gabrielle. Something about her made me uneasy, and I have addressed this with Ant on many occasions. He would tell me that I am tripping and had nothing to worry about.

If that was really the case, why the HELL is she contacting my husband to wake him up. I couldn't tell him that I seen the message though because then he would know that I checked his phone.

"Baby, can you get me a towel," Anthony called out interrupting all thoughts of Gabrielle.

I wanted to say something so badly, but my heart wouldn't let me.

I got up and rushed around the room trying to help him finish getting ready. I knew that I had to play my part and make him see that I am the perfect wife for him at all times.

When I stop by for lunch, I am going to have to casually inform Ms. Gabrielle, that I am the ONLY one that will give him early morning wake up calls.

After Anthony left, I went back to sleep for a couple of hours. A quarter to ten, I jumped up by the sound of my phone ringing.

"Hey girl, what's up?" Kim, my best friend asked me. We have been friends ever since Anthony and I moved to New Jersey almost five years ago.

"What time is it?" I asked feeling somewhat delirious. I told Anthony that I was going to meet him for lunch, but I needed to hurry if I was going to be showered, dressed, and at his office by 11:30.

Ding-Dong, chimed my doorbell.

"Kim, someone is at my door, and I have to hurry and get dressed to meet my baby. Give me a minute; I will call you in the car." I quickly told her, putting on my robe.

I dropped my phone on the bed, and hurried down the stairs.

"Just a minute!" I yelled out rushing to the door. I looked out the peep hole and seen an officer on the other side of my door.

"Why in the hell is the police here?" I said softly under my breath and flung the door open. In my past the only times the police came to your door was to give you bad news, so all kind of foolishness ran through my mind.

"Yes." I asked the officer tugging my robe close. My heart was thumping in my chest as I waited for the officer to respond.

"Lisa Oliver?" he asked me while thumbing through his pile.

"Yes. I am Lisa Oliver. How can I help you," I asked him waiting in suspense. It felt like forever as he handed me the documents.

"You officially have been served," he informed me handing me a packet.

Quickly he turned and walked back to the sheriff's car and hopped in. Frozen in my spot, I felt myself getting weak as I read through the documents.

"Divorce!!! Anthony is divorcing me," I said aloud not to anyone in particular. Suddenly I felt faint as everything around me began to spin.

The last thing I remembered was my neighbor saying good morning, before I hit the floor. All of a sudden, everything went black.

Closure

Anthony

"Your wife has been served Ant," my attorney Maxwell informed me. I was sitting at my desk, and let out a sigh of relief. I have been waiting for this moment for a while, and I really didn't exactly know how I was supposed to respond.

Keeping up this charade for as long as I had too has been difficult, and I am glad that I can stop pretending to like this woman. I had to keep my cool, and play my position if my plan was going to be executed the way that I wanted it too.

"So what's next?" I asked Maxwell gripping my stress ball with my left hand.

Ever since I decided to divorce Lisa, I have been on edge. I wanted this to be over as quickly as it started, but I have to be cautious of what may happen next.

"Are you going home tonight?" A sweet voice interrupted my conversation.

"Max, let me give you a call back," I said rushing off the phone. Setting the handset down on the receiver, I turned my attention to my office doorway.

A look of concern was written all over Gabrielle's delicate face. She has been such a support system to me these past couple of weeks, for which I will be forever grateful.

The day that Gabrielle started, was the day that Michael, my private investigator, dropped the bomb on me, letting me know all about my wife's secret life.

Gabrielle was already nervous because I am a stickler for perfection, but I do not do well with the training process. I was trying to ensure that Nadia was going to be around to train her, but the world is not perfect when it comes to me. Nadia went into premature labor with her twins, leaving Gabrielle all alone on her second day.

I was nervous, which made me mean to everyone. Softly Gabrielle knocked on the door, to inform me that I had a visitor. I knew who it was already but Gabrielle wasn't aware.

"You have a visitor Mr. Oliv- -," Gabrielle started, but I didn't even give her a chance to finish.

"Just let him in, and stay in your place!" I barked at her, making her uneasy. I was so scared of the information that Michael was going to give me.

I know it seems crazy that I hired a private investigator to dig up information on my wife, but my Momma always told me to go with your gut feeling. God gives us signs when we least expect it, and when the incident happened in Baltimore six months ago, I can

15

honestly say that it was something that I did not expect.

My mother lives in Annapolis, Maryland, but ever since Lisa and I got married, we always stayed in the Harbor and enjoyed the culture that the city of Baltimore had to offer.

Well, that was partly the reason why we always stayed in the Harbor. The main reason was that my Mother has never liked Lisa.

My mother, Elizabeth Oliver, came from a long lineage of strong black women that held their family down, so of course she wanted me to be with another woman of color that would do the same thing, but truth be told, it was way deeper than that.

My father started cheating on my mother with his assistant, a dingy blonde named Sharon not long after I was born. It wasn't until I was an adult that my mother informed me that she always knew about this affair, and the long list of mistresses that he had in the cities he frequented on business.

"These women fulfilled a void for your father," my mother told me one day when she was visiting me in college. "First of all, I couldn't just pack up and follow him everywhere he went, especially when we had you boys at home. I wanted to focus on getting my career in order in case I would ever have to take care of myself and my children.

I love you boys, but I wish I waited before having four of you back to back. I gave you boys the attention that your father was in need of, and I can honestly admit that.

I need you to promise me that once you get married, you turn to your wife, and not any random chick on the side. That way, you won't need to get attention from a third party."

Out of all the lessons that my mother taught me, those words stood out the most. It made complete sense. That is why when I found out that Lisa was pregnant when we got together; I quickly paid for the abortion.

It was already bad enough that I was in love with a white woman, but a pregnant one?

That was not going to fly with my mother, especially after the last white woman that came into her family life and was the mother of my illegitimate half brother, Anthony III.

Mom knew about my father's affair for many years and dealt with it; but it wasn't until she found out about my *half* brother, that she officially despised seeing a black man with a white woman and asked my father for a divorce.

This is why when I decided that I was going to marry Lisa; I had to make sure that she was perfect all the way around. I couldn't allow her to meet my family being *pregnant*. My mother would have had a field day with that information.

Instead, I did what any young rational man in love would do. I paid for an abortion, nursed her back to health, and gave her unconditional love promising her that once we were married, we can start our own family.

The day that I brought Lisa home to meet my mother, a dark cloud hung over our relationship. That is also when I stopped staying at my mother's five thousand square foot home, and started utilizing the hotels inside the Harbor of Baltimore whenever we were in the area.

Now, the day that I started doubting the substance of my marriage; Lisa, my brother Malcolm, my Mother, and I were having lunch in Little Italy. We were barely seated when the server came out handing each of us the wine menu.

When Lisa looked up and thanked him for the menu, a large gasp rose up from the server's throat. He dropped his pen and pad, and stood staring at her as if he seen a ghost.

"Monica, is that you," the young man asked barely over a whisper.

Lisa being mistaken for someone else wasn't unusual, so if my mother wasn't there, I probably would not have paid it any attention. Folks have always thought she was Ali Larter or Sarah Carter. My wife was beautiful, and she put a lot of time and energy into making sure that she was flawless at all times.

I knew that my Mother was going to have something smart to say about the matter, so I turned my attention to my wife, to shoot her a look of apologies, but it was the reaction of my wife that sent a chill throughout my body.

Her body tensed up, and she took in a couple of deep breaths. Lisa didn't respond. She kept her cool, but I did see a look of panic briefly run across her face. It only lasted for a moments because she quickly got it together.

A Cold Piece

Laughing nervously, Lisa looked the waiter directly in the eye and said, "My name is not Monica. I am sorry that you have me mistaken. May I give you my wine order now?"

Everyone was silent as we waited for him to respond. Quickly he apologized and rushed away from the table leaving the pad and pen on the ground a few inches from Lisa's feet.

Another waitress, was watching the entire exchange, and rushed over completing our order.

There was an air of un-comfortableness that loomed over our table, and everyone felt it. Well everyone except Lisa.

She carried herself throughout the duration of the meal as if nothing ever happened; laughing and telling us about the fundraising project that she was working on. I kept looking around for that waiter, but I did not see him on the floor anywhere.

21

Driving back to my mother's, I was silent and was lost in deep thought.

Who is Monica? Where did the waiter go? Why did my wife look as if she seen a ghost when he called her Monica?

My mother must have been thinking the same thing, because once I returned to my office the following week, there was a message on my voicemail from her with Michael's information, her personal private investigator.

This is why I retained Michael to find out as much about my wife's past as possible, and follow her around.

I was appalled after learning that my wife was not the person I thought she was. Her real name was indeed Monica, Monica Davis, and was currently wanted for questioning in regards to her ex-boyfriend's murder in Minnesota.

Michael also informed me that while I was at work, my wife was gallivanting around town with as many college boys that she could fit into her weekly schedule. Using my money to wine and dine the punks.

What do you do after you find out information like that? Come home and demand her to give me a divorce?

No. You have to come up with an immaculate exit plan. I didn't have anyone to confide in outside of my family, and I needed as much emotional support as possible. It was during this time that Gabrielle and I grew closer.

Unlike Lisa, Gabrielle's spirit was so warm and inviting. Every day she made sure that I was okay, and ensured me that the situation would be over before we knew it.

"I will be okay Gabby, but only if you do one thing." I informed her motioning for her come in my office.

Closing the door behind her, a warm smile developed across her face as she asked me, "What do you need me to do?"

"Baby girl, can you please give me a hug? That is all that I need from you right now." I stood up as tears escaped the corners of my eyes, opening my arms welcoming her over.

Nodding her head yes, Gabrielle rushed into my arms giving me the warmest hug that I have ever felt in my life.

Disbelief

Lisa

I don't know how long I was unconscious for, but I woke up with Mrs. Garner, my nosy neighbor from across the street, standing over me trying to revive me.

"Oh my goodness, Lisa!" she exclaimed as I finally came to. "What the heck is going on? First the police is at your door, and moments later you are passed out on the foyer. Is everything okay? Did something happen to Anthony?"

Anthony!

The very mention of his name made me remember everything that just happened.

"Um, Mrs. Garner, I am okay, just not feeling too well that's all," I quickly explained hoping that she did not get a glimpse of the divorce papers spread out on the floor.

Quickly getting up, I flashed her a shaky smile attempting to reassure her that I was okay. I needed her to leave so that I could gather my thoughts. I needed to speak to my husband and not over the phone. This shit had to be a mistake. Why would he be filing for a divorce? We just made powerful love this morning. This had to be a mistake.

"You sure honey?" she questioned not looking too convinced.

"Yes, Mrs. Garner I am sure. I am not trying to be rude, but I need to hurry and get dressed. I have an appointment and I need to get out of here. Thank you again for checking on me." I said while inching my front door closed.

I was starting to lose my composure, and if she didn't leave she was going to be introduced to the old Lisa. The one that I kept bottled up and tucked away. The one that I promised myself that I would never let come back to life ever since I met my husband.

"Okay dear," Mrs. Garner told me. "I am here if you need me, okay?"

I quickly nodded yes, and closed my front door. Rushing up the stairs I threw on a sun dress and sandals. Typically, I would have brushed my long blonde tresses one hundred times and professionally applied my make up, but this was not the time.

I had to get my marriage back, and the bad thing is that I didn't know why the hell it was in jeopardy.

"Archie! What is going on? I need to speak to my husband," I informed the head of security. I barely had a chance to park my car correctly before Archie and his goon squad met me outside, informing me that I was not allowed into the building.

"I am sorry Mrs. Oliver," Archie said flashing me a look of pity. He was speaking to me in the middle of the street while the rest of the men in black blocked the entrance way, and spoke to each other on their walkie-talkies.

"You cannot, come in the building ma' am." Archie shook his head and stayed firm. "I do apologize, but I have strict orders from Mr. Oliver that you cannot go into the building."

I stood in disbelief that all this was happening to me, with questions racing through in my mind. Anthony didn't want to see me? He was divorcing me? What the hell happened that caused all of this? What the hell did I do wrong?

Tears started to creep down my face as I stood frozen in the street.

A Cold Piece

"Mrs. Oliver, I am sorry to do this, but I have to ask you to leave," Archie said to me but his voice started to fade away. For the second time today, I felt everything around me go black.

Six months later......

Decisions

Lisa

3:04 AM. That is what time the clock on my I-phone read. I looked out the window then back down at my phone.

"Should I call her?" I asked myself under my breath, "or should I call him?"

Gripping the phone with my left hand, I rubbed the beads of sweat off of my forehead with my right. I felt like a convict waiting to get out of solitaire confinement. I turned the light switch on, continuing to stare at my phone.

I dialed three digits of his number and hung up. "I know that they are together, and he is not going to answer," I said to myself under my breath, shaking my head. I stood up and walked over to the pantry.

Hidden inside of my Cookie Monster Cookie Jar, was the number of the one person that I knew was the cause of my living nightmare. The one person that played enough mind games to get my husband to do exactly what she wanted him to do and that was to divorce me.

The last six months has been hell for me. I kept hope alive up until the day that the judge pronounced us divorce. I had to admit that Anthony made everything so easy for me. He left me the house, my two cars, and one hundred thousand dollars.

I didn't fight him for anything, because I refused to believe that our marriage was really over. It wasn't until I was all alone in my ten thousand square foot home, and the electricity was shut off, that the reality of what was happening came to me.

A Cold Piece

Not only did my husband abandon me, he had the audacity to turn off all the utilities that were in his name. It took me almost a week and a half to even have enough energy to call the electric company and find out what did I have to do to turn it back on in my own name.

Kim would stop by periodically to check on me, but I seemed to be taking a turn for the worst. She would force me to eat a couple of bites whenever she was around and take in a couple of sips of water.

Alone. I still cannot believe that I am alone. This divorce made me feel like I was unworthy of compassion and love. Kim tried to reassure me that we must have grown apart, but I didn't believe that shit. The only way that a man can fall out of love with you with such force, is if someone promised him that she can love him better.

I have not been able to eat or sleep. I have lost so much weight, and my hair was limp. I wanted my family back and I wanted it now! This was the final straw, and I promise Anthony and her that I am not a force to be reckoned with or underestimated.

I have been begging Anthony for an answer to why he left, and he still won't talk to me. The only means of communication that I have had with him has been through his attorney.

I have been having a fit, trying to figure out what happened between us making passionate, hot love one moment, to me alone with no husband the next.

I left so many messages on his voicemail, begging him to come home. I needed my husband. I was all Anthony needed, and I had to come up with a plan to make him see that.

Sprawled across the floor in my kitchen, I dropped my phone on the ground and curled up in a ball. I wasn't going to call that BITCH. I had to show both of them that I was the bigger person.

I know I may seem irrational and sporadic, but who wouldn't be if they knew for a fact that their mate has moved on without even letting you know why.

I closed my eyes as the tears flowed from my eyes. I can't keep feeling this way. I had to start thinking with my head because allowing my heart to lead is what got me into this situation.

I had dreams of my husband every night. I craved his touch on the small of my back. He was my savior, my rock and I never questioned his judgment. Ever since I met Anthony, I have left my entire life in the palm of his hands.

I followed him wherever he led me, because I knew that eventually letting him have control of everything would finally allow me to have the one thing that I wanted. My baby. Anthony promised me that.

I begged him on so many occasions to not break my heart. I have been through so much in the past and was determined to have stability. I let my guard down. I can honestly admit that I was not physically and/or mentally prepared for this divorce.

Anthony led me on to the very end. Like I said before, his patience was a virtue. He played chess with my emotions. He took my pure love that I had for him, and was convinced that it was dirty.

I yearned to relive the last moment that we had sex. Whenever I closed my eyes, I could still feel my husband inside of me. The way he touched me, mmmm... he possessed so much power within those hands.

All I wanted from my husband was love. I believed in my heart that we possessed true love. In the beginning I was so scared that I would lose this perfect man. He showed me on so many occasions that he loved me unconditionally, and was not going anywhere.

Ugh! I wonder if seeing Eric caused this? I thought to myself sitting up. A chill ran down the small of my back as I tried to remember everything that happened that day in Baltimore when Eric, my ex fiancé' brother, recognized me.

No, that couldn't be it. I played it off cool. Matter of fact, Anthony didn't even bring it back up. Maybe Mother Elizabeth brought it back up to him.

I felt a panic attack coming on, and I jumped up gasping for air. That old biddy better not be the reason why I am all alone. She kept her eyes glued on me the entire time that Eric spoke to me. It was like she was trying to read in between the lines of my facial expressions.

Clutching my counter top, I took in several deep breaths trying to calm myself down. That was the other reason why I didn't fight Anthony in court. I didn't want Maxwell, his powerhouse attorney to pull up anything about my past.

I did an excellent job recreating myself into Lisa, the perfect stay at home wife. The one that longed to produce a son for my husband, the one that made sure that her hair was immaculate at all times.

I did a perfect job bottling up Monica; the weak, sensitive, attention seeking woman of my past. No one could ever find out about my prior relationship with Leonard Grant, and my involvement in his death or Darrin's disappearance.

I am going crazy trying to decipher what the hell happened. I took a couple more deep breaths and decided that I needed to pay Eric and Mother Elizabeth a little visit if I was going to be able to get my husband back.

Two years later.

Did My Water Just Break?

Gabrielle

"Babe, what time do you want to meet for dinner?" I spoke into the phone as Andrice, my best friend, beckoned the waitress over for our check. We spent the morning shopping on Rodeo Drive for the right wraps and jewelry for my pregnancy portraits tomorrow.

Even though my doctor didn't approve, I was in Los Angeles to allow Mello, one my husband's best friends, to capture the beauty of my pregnant belly.

A Cold Piece

I was a week shy of being eight months pregnant, but I felt great. When Anthony informed me that he had to come to the west coast, I jumped at the opportunity to schedule a session with Mello, and have a couple of my girl friends come along to keep me company as he worked.

"Escucha mi amor, yo estoy en mi camino. Prefiero morir, que no esté con usted. Te amo.ent." Anthony whispered sweet nothings into the phone making the heat between my legs increase.

I loved the way that my husband was so well rounded. He spoke three languages which included my native tongue of Spanish.

Anthony had a meeting that morning, so Dricie, Loretta, Monique, and 1 decided to hang out. We started the morning off with shopping, stopped by the Pacific Seafood Grill for lunch, and were going to wrap it up with massages and facials back at our hotel.

"Mrs. Oliver, I promise that I will be there before you know it." Anthony reassured me gently.

"Okay," I replied as a smile crept up the corners of my mouth. Anthony knew all he had to do was call me Mrs. Oliver, and I melted like butter.

"Stop cup caking and get off the phone," my feisty friend Loretta fussed from across the table. "We are supposed to be enjoying our girl time. Blow him a kiss and say good-bye baby. Sheesh." She blew out and playfully rolled her eyes.

"Okay baby. I will see you tonight," I said softly into the receiver. I blew him a kiss and hung up the phone laughing.

"Girl! You are so silly," I laughed playfully tossing my napkin in her direction.

I pulled out my card and slid it across the table to Andrice. "Since you ladies have waited on me hand and foot all day today, I guess I can return the favor and pay for lunch." I laughed rubbing my belly.

I had such a wonderful group of girlfriends. We were such a diverse group, but so much alike.

Monique was a Thai and black mixed woman with a small build and extremely sophisticated, who wore her hair short. She possessed such a beautiful spirit and would give you the shirt off of her back if you needed it. Monique actually moved to Los Angeles about a year ago after she married Mello. They met at our engagement party, and he fell in love with my friend the moment he laid eyes on her.

He not only courted Monique, but he courted her two girls, Lyric and Justice as well. He was their knight in shining armor and she knew it. When Mello finally popped the question, my girl didn't hesitate to say yes. They had an intimate wedding in our home, and soon after, Mello relocated her and the girls to California.

Andrice, who was my best friend, stood almost six foot tall barefoot. She was a dark skinned sistah with beautiful shoulder length sister locks who recently relocated to Newark, New Jersey to teach third grade at an exclusive private school.

I have known Monique and Andrice ever since I moved to the east coast almost ten years ago. Since my father was my only living relative, these two ladies quickly became the sisters that I never had.

Finally, there is Loretta. Lo Lo, (as we call her) was the final piece to our mixed up puzzle. She was also Latina; with roots stemming from Puerto Rico and was thick in all of the right places with long wavy jet black hair. Lo Lo came into our lives by accident, and I mean that literally.

Monique's children's father was also the father of Lo Lo's seven year old twin boys,

44

Michael and Robert. Neither one of the women knew about each other. Well, let me take that back. Monique didn't know about Loretta, but Lo Lo had a feeling that Michael was still messing with his other "baby mama."

One day, Loretta popped up at the apartment that Monique and I shared, pushing a stroller with the most adorable little boys that I had ever seen. I don't know what her original mission was, but by the end of the night, after an abundance of tears she was silently initiated into our group.

"Well Mommy, if you are taking care of the meal, the least we can do is leave the tip," Loretta said nodding at the others to follow her lead and get some cash out of their purses.

Once outside the restaurant, Monique handed the valet attendant her ticket. "Damn, it's almost two o'clock? I have to hurry and get the girls from school. Do you ladies mind taking a cab back to the hotel?

"No mamacita, you are good. Take care of your business. No one wants to have a set of ten year old twins waiting by themselves, especially my babies." I leaned in and kissed Mo's cheek.

We all took turns giving Monique quick kisses as the valet driver pulled up in her black Land Rover.

"Ms. Jones?" he asked holding the door open. Monique gave him her ticket stub and a twenty dollar bill.

"Yes, that's me," she responded flashing him a smile and getting settled into the driver's seat.

"You may want to get your brakes checked out. I had to tap on them a couple of times to stop. You may just have air in them." He informed her, shutting the door behind her.

Monique rolled down the window, and handed the young brother another ten.

46

"Thank you for the information. I will have my husband check it out as soon as I get home."

Waving at us she said "chao ladies. See you tonight for dinner," and turned up her radio. The sound of Adele crooned through her speakers as she merged into traffic.

"Do you ladies need a cab?" the attendant asked Loretta. She informed him that we did, and he stood in the street hailing one over.

I kept my eyes on Monique's truck with a slight smile on my face. I was so happy for her. So much has changed for her since Mello came into her life. She didn't have to worry about struggling anymore.

Mello took her out of her two bedroom apartment in Jersey City to a baby mansion on the hills of Malibu. The girls loved him and welcomed him in as their new father. He accepted her children as his own, and they were even in the process of him adopting them.

What more could you ask for? I thought to myself.

What happened next, I was not prepared for. I could see that Monique's brake lights were flashing on and off but her truck continued at the same speed as she approached the intersection. Her light changed to red, but by the frantic motion of her brake lights, I could see that she did not have any control of her truck.

I grabbed my belly with my left hand and started running in her direction, waving my right arm in the air. I tried to scream, but the sound just would not come out. I could hear the yells of Loretta and Andrice behind me as I continued to run down the street.

A garbage truck was hurling in the direction of Monique's truck at full speed. It felt like an eternity, but I watched as the truck ran head first into the driver side of her vehicle. I could hear the blood curling sound of the metal impacting metal.

I fell to my knees as I watched her SUV flip over several times as the garbage truck turned over onto its left side. Several of the valet attendants darted past me, as others closer to the intersection tried to save my friend.

The scream that I was so hard trying to release, finally escaped my throat as I watched the scene in horror. I closed my eyes praying to the Lord that I was dreaming and he would allow me to wake up.

I felt my limp body being pulled up into a standing position. I couldn't bear to open my eyes. I wanted to rewind time back to us being inside of the restaurant. I wanted us to exit again laughing and chattering waiting for the valet attendant. I wanted to hear him give her his warning again about her brakes. I wanted to tell her to leave the truck right there, and let Mello get it towed to the nearest garage.

I wanted to do so much, but I couldn't. It was too late. My friend was gone, and there was nothing that I could do about it. I could hear the sirens getting closer.

"HELP!" I heard Loretta's shrill voice scream out into the crowd. "Somebody, please get us an ambulance my friend's water broke, and she is in labor!"

Labor? What is she talking about? I thought to myself while opening my eyes. I glanced down between my legs, and I seen a mixture of blood and water smeared on the sidewalk.

Did my water just break?

Loretta and a man that I could not identify were trying to help me. Andrice was nowhere in sight, but I figured she must have been trying to help Monique.

Moments later, I felt my body being lifted into the air, and placed upon a stretcher.

"Ma'am, are you okay? You have lost a lot of blood. How many fingers do I have up?"

A Cold Piece

The young paramedic asked me. I turned my head to the left trying to find Loretta, and I felt goose bumps run up and down the length of my arms.

Oh my gosh! I thought to myself. Was that Lisa? A dark haired woman with glasses was staring at me intensely.

"LO!" I screamed out frantically trying to find my friend. "I am right here baby, I am right behind you. Shhhh calm down. I am trying to call Anthony."

I glanced back in the direction of where I thought I seen Lisa, but the woman was nowhere to be found.

A Big Mistake

Lisa

Damn, I'm spoiled! I thought to myself as I tried to find a seat on this crowded Grey Hound bus.

I hated public transportation, but I had to come up with a plan to get back and forth that was untraceable. There was no way that I could explain being in California the same time that the love birds were there as well.

The bus reeked of cigarettes and vapor rub. The sounds of crying babies, obnoxious cell phone conversations, and laughter could be heard throughout the vehicle. This is going to be a hell of a ride, but I had no choice.

My eyes scanned each row for an empty seat, but I did not locate one. I was about to pay someone for their seat when I heard a deep voice come from the back of the bus. "Sweetness, there's a seat back here."

A heavy set man was waving to me from the very last seat of the bus. From where I was standing, it did not look like the seat next him was empty, but the closer that I got to him, I could see there was. The man took up his seat and half of what would be mine, but at this point it did not matter.

There was no way that I could get my butt off this bus and wait on the next one because I know for a fact that Gabrielle recognized me. I looked her dead in the eye and watched the look of fear and disbelief rush across her face as the EMT's prepped her for departure. I could not risk getting caught up, with my plan having not been accomplished.

"Beggars can't be choosers," I mumbled under my breath, making my way to the back of the bus. I flashed the man a quick smile, and struggled to squeeze past him.

"Thank you so much, I thought I was going to have to get off the bus," I informed him trying hard not to gasp. The odor that seeped from his pores was atrocious, and I wasn't sure if I was going to be able to last for the two day ride.

Hopefully, he is not going as far as I am. I was trying to get back to Jersey quick, fast and in a hurry. I needed to come up with another game plan.

I turned my attention to the window as I felt the bus begin to slowly move forward. I could feel the tears building up in my eyes, but I promised myself that I would not shed one fucking tear behind the two of them and what they had going on. Seeing Gabrielle

54

pregnant sparked a nerve that I knew would not go out until she was out of the picture.

The loud intercom came on as the bus driver informed us of the rules and regulations of riding the bus. I could barely hear exactly what he was saying due to the static but it was okay. I was lost in thought coming up with a plan B to getting rid of Gabrielle and getting my man back.

From the Pen of *Nicola*

Scared

Anthony

Tick. Tock. Tick. Tock. Beep. Beep.

I was trying to sleep on the little fold out bed that sat bedside Gabrielle's hospital bed. The sounds of all of the machines around me kept me up. Finally Gabrielle was asleep, but I know not peacefully. What mother would be able to rest after an ordeal like that?

I rubbed my fingertips over her delicate left hand, silently saying a prayer. I was so happy that my wife finally calmed down. The medical staff had to sedate her before giving her the emergency c-section. She was hysterical from witnessing her friend's death and knowing that she was going to have to deliver her son a whole month early.

"I seen her baby, I seen her!" was all that she kept screaming. "It was all her fault. Lisa tried to kill me. Mo is dead because of me! Lisa was trying to kill me!" It took four nurses to hold her down as the doctor injected medicine into her IV.

"Shhh baby... It's okay," I crooned trying to calm her down. Part of me wanted to believe that Gabby was just traumatized and over reacting; but something in my gut told me otherwise. Why would she make up such a thing and blame it on Lisa?

It was going on two years, and we have not heard anything at all from Lisa. At first, after the divorce, she called constantly begging me to come back. In her head, she believed that Gabrielle was the reason why I left her, but that was totally not the case.

58

It was all the information that I learned from the private investigator that made it clear to me that I needed to head for the hills and quickly. My relationship with Gabby grew after our separation. She made sure that I ate and that I was mentally okay. She called me every day and would tell me that everything was going to be alright. She was my rock, and I had to repay her by making her my wife. I finally found real, unconditional love, and I was not going to let anyone come in between us.

Forty-five minutes later, the doctor pulled my tiny son's body out of Gabby's stomach, quickly handing him over to the pediatric nursing staff that was waiting to pounce into action. The crew quickly cleared out his mouth and nasal passages, as the doctor cut his umbilical cord. I stood on the sidelines in awe watching them carefully handle this tiny being. While wiping the cream colored substance off of his body, the crew quickly weighed and measured him.

Finally the sound that we have all been waiting for rang out in the operating room. The baby's soft cry sounded like music to my ears. One of the nurses smiled at me as she wrapped him up into a blanket. Another pulled a tiny stripped hat onto his head.

"Are you ready to hold your son?" the first nurse, whose name tag said Brenda asked me nodding for me to come in closer. I never held a baby that small, and I was scared to death. "He seems to be doing okay, but we need to take him to the Pediatric Intensive Care Ward to make sure that he is good since he is only four pounds, 3 ounces." Tears escaped the corners of my eyes as I took in a couple of deep breaths, and nodded yes. I put one hand under his head, and the other hand under his rump.

"Hey little man," I whispered to my son. I couldn't do anything else but stare at him. He was so beautiful! At first glance you could see the resemblance to his mother, but there was no doubt that this was my son. He had my exact face!

It felt as if no one else was in the room as I stared and crooned at the new addition to my family. I prayed over him asking the Lord to protect him from any unnecessary evils that the world may produce. I prayed that the Lord would protect my entire family from whatever may be going on.

I kissed my son on the head and handed him back over to the nurse. I watched as she gently unwrapped him and placed an identification bracelet onto his ankle. "Your wife has the same exact one on her arm. This allows us to know that this is your baby. It also has an alarm on it so that if by any chance someone was to try and take him off of this floor, an alarm will go off throughout the hospital and all of the entrances will lock down."

I looked Brenda square in the eyes and thanked her. "Please take care of him," I asked her trying hard to hold back the fresh set of tears that was threatening to be released.

She flashed me a reassuring smile, nodding her head. "We sure will Mr. Oliver. You can trust and believe that."

Gently she placed my son into a portable crib and informed the other nurses that it was time to go. One of them held the door open, while the others gathered up all of their equipment.

"Mr. Oliver, did you and your wife decide on his name?" she asked me as she neared the door. "We try to address each baby by their name, not baby boy Smith, or baby girl Jones."

A soft smile twitched in the corners of my mouth as I proudly told her the name that Gabby and I have agreed on. "His name is A.J., which stands for Anthony Vashawn Oliver Jr."

All the nurses smiled at me as they felt the level of happiness radiate from me.

"That is a beautiful name sir," Brenda said smiling down at my son. "Okay AJ, Ms. Brenda and her team promises you that we are going to take good care of you, so that you can hurry home with your Mommy and Daddy."

I waved good bye to the crew as they exited the room and turned my attention back to my sleeping wife. The surgical technicians were about done cleaning her up from the c-section. That is when the reality of what was going on really hit me.

Gabby just had a major surgery performed on her, and was oblivious to it all. The moment that I witnessed my son emerging from her body, I forgot all about her, and could only see his face. Is this what they meant by the term, love is blind?

"Is she going to be okay?" I asked the nurse that was taking her vital signs. The selfish side of me wanted my wife to wake up and bask in the moment of being a proud parent with me, but the logical part of me knew that it was best for her to sleep.

"As of right now, it looks like it, but it is still hard to say. She has been through a lot today sir, so for the most part, it is best for her to sleep it off. Let her build up her energy. Once the doctor comes back in the morning and checks her out, he can give you a better answer that I can."

I respected her response and waited patiently as the crew cleaned up my wife, and prepared to move her out of the operating room and into a private room. I removed the garments that the nurses made me put on over my clothes for surgery and gathered all of our belongings.

It wasn't until we departed the room that I remembered that we were not in this hospital alone. Andrice, Loretta, Mello, his mother and the twins were all inside the cramped waiting room. An uneasy sense of sadness and joy loomed throughout the room.

"We are taking her to room 336 in post partum," one of the nurses informed me. "Take your time with your family. Your wife is in good hands."

She flashed us a quick smile as they continued their trek down the hallway. After a pregnant pause, Andrice finally stood up and gave me a hug.

"We got to see the baby," she said barely over a whisper. "He looks just like you."

We continued to hold each other as the others stood and joined our embrace. Everyone bid me congratulations, but you could tell their hearts were not in it. It was a bittersweet moment for us all, gaining a new addition, but loosing such a great one the same day.

Several hours later, I was alone in the room with my wife, and she was still sound asleep. I checked my phone, and seen that I had a text from Loretta. It said; *When you get everything settled, call me....*

I will call her in the morning. Right now, I just had to be sure, that my wife was going to be okay. I was scared to death.

Did Lisa really do this? If so, why is she after my wife?

I bowed my head and prayed that God would help me see the truth, and protect my family.

Same Routine

Lisa

"Hello, my name is Tilly Davidson, and I wanted to know if the Oliver family still utilized your staffing agency for holiday work? I temped with your company for them about two years ago, and I just loved the atmosphere! If you do, Can I give you my updated information so that I can be one of the first ones for that assignment?"

The young lady on the other end jotted down my information and asked me to hold as she updated Tilly's file with my information. I went into the parlor and sat down Indian style on the floor in front of the coffee table. There were so many papers sprawled across the table, that a person with OCD would have gone crazy, but too me, it was organized.

"Okay Tilly, your file has been updated. I see there is a star by your name too so you were automatically on the list for us to check for availability for this assignment. Since you are already registered and we are updating your information now, you don't have to come by the office until after the assignment to pick up your check. Expect to hear from us a week before Thanksgiving. Thanks Tilly!" The bubbly receptionist informed me.

Shaking my head, I tossed my phone onto the couch, and turned my attention back to the documents on the table. I wanted it to appear cluttered, so when Kim and/or one of my male friends that occasionally stopped by became nosey, they would have to know how to crack Morse code to understand the method to my madness.

A Cold Piece

I don't know if it is a completely bad thing that my husband was a creature of habit. He was the ultimate believer in that if it ain't broke, don't fix it. He has been using this agency ever since we moved to Jersey City to staff our home for Thanksgiving and Christmas. The agency would send cooks, waiters/waitresses, and a cleaning crew to prepare and serve the guest before, during and after the holiday celebration.

I knew that there was a star by Tilly's name, because I always filled out a comment card in regards to her. She always did a great job, and I even requested Anthony to hire her full time as a maid in our home. He promised me that the moment that we both decided the time was right for us to start a family that he would bring Tilly on. This is why I kept in contact with Tilly directly. I called her once every couple of months to check on her, and see if she was still interested in working for us.

After the divorce, I continued to call her because I knew that our separation was only for the moment, and that my husband was going to wake up, smell the roses, and come back home so that we can work on our family again. The last time we spoke though, Tilly informed me that she was going to move to Arizona to take care of her father. He was diagnosed with kidney cancer and required the extra care.

I pulled out a notebook from the bottom of the pile and flipped through the pages, until I reached an itemized check list. I checked off, contact agency. The next item on the list was, pay my husband a visit. Yes, when we took our vows we promised each other till death do us part, and at this point that is the only thing that I was going to let happen to *keep* us apart.

I tucked my notebook away and pressed play on my DVD player. I had the best of "Gilligan's Island" in the player and fell asleep on it last night. Yes! This is what my world has come too. No cable, watching old movies on video, and planning on getting Anthony back. Some would think that I seemed miserable, but I am not. I am actually proud of myself. I am standing up and fighting to get my family back.

Lying down on the floor, I closed my eyes and rolled onto my back. Visions of Anthony appeared in my head as I ran my fingertips underneath the sheer fabric of my t-shirt until I reached my breast. Softly I ran circles around each of them, brushing my areola back and forth my thumb. This is the way that Anthony always touched me, and I tried my hardest to implement his touch. By the end of the year, the REAL Mr. and Mrs. Oliver will be back together and Gabrielle will be a distant memory in his system. I promise you that.

From the Pen of *Nicola*

A Rude Awakening

Anthony

"I am about to head out now Mr. Oliver, is there anything else that you need me to do before I go?" David, my assistant asked me through our internal intercom system. We have been working like slaves on a plantation for the last couple of days, and it was starting to take a toll on all of us. Gabrielle included.

"The only thing I need you to do is confirm my reservations for tonight, and then we are good," I responded. I was about done with my to do list for the day, so I prepared to head out myself. Gabby has been complaining that ever since our son came home, it seems as if I have become busier than ever.

"Your reservation has been confirmed sir. I will see you in the morning. Have a good night." I could hear David shutting down outside my door, and moments later, I seen the light in his area go dim. I got up and gathered my brief case, jacket and scarf.

Trying to gain a balance between being a businessman, a husband, and now a father has been a struggle, but just like that old saying of "Only the Strong Survive," I have to make sure I come out on top and not fall to the waist side like my father did. I promised my wife, myself, and my mother, God rest her soul, that I was not going to lose focus and would make the necessary adjustments in my life.

Just thinking of my wife and son brought a smile to my face. Gabrielle was such a light that took on the role of motherhood just as gracefully as my own mother did when she managed us growing up. Once her own strength was built up, my wife assisted the medical staff at the hospital in nursing AJ to gain another pound and was eligible to go home. Even though the loss of Monique has been hindering her, Gabrielle turned that negative into a positive. She declared that Mo was AJ's personal angel protecting and watching over him.

AJ was so strong. If you didn't know that he was a preemie at birth, you sure in the hell were not able to tell now. That little boy was such a firecracker. He has formed his own identity at only three months old. He listens to you with such an inquisitive look on his little face; it was as if he knew exactly what you were talking about. I knew that my mother would have been so proud of our bundle of joy. He had my exact face.

I turned off the light in my office and opened the door. I nearly jumped out of my skin finding out that I was not alone. The hairs on the back of my neck stood straight up and goose bumps ran up and down the lengths of both my arms. Lisa was standing there with her right arm raised in a knocking position.

"Wha- wha-, what are you doing here?" I asked her. I haven't seen Lisa in over two years, and I was trying to keep it like that. I just recently got Gabrielle to stop talking about her, and now here she is standing right in front of me. She was still beautiful, but there was something different about her. Something in her eyes made me feel eerie.

"Awe baby," Lisa said gradually running her hand down my chest. "Is that the way you greet your wife Anthony?" She stood on her tip toes and kissed my cheek. Her intimate gesture startled me, making me take a couple of steps back into my office.

That is all Lisa needed as in invitation. Before I knew it, she closed the door with her foot, while unbuckling my pants. My heart was beating uncontrollably. I felt as if I was having an outer body experience. I wanted to push her away from me, tell her to stay the hell away from me and my family; but the words were stuck. Within moments, Lisa fell to her knees, pulled my johnson out of my pants, and into her mouth.

My eyes rolled to the back of my head as the memories of our good times raced through my mind. I dropped everything that I was carrying and leaned back against my desk. The way she ran her tongue down the perimeter of my dick, made my toes curl. Lisa took her time with every motion, making it suddenly hot as hell in my office. One thing that we never lacked in our relationship was sex. Lisa knew exactly what to do to make me cum over and over again. It wasn't until she moaned and called my name out, that I started to come back to my senses.

"Lisa! Stop it!"

I pulled my dick out of her mouth and quickly tried to get myself together.

"You BITCH!" I spat at her, tucking my shirt into my pants. "You are not my wife! What the hell are you doing here?" I was panting, damn near hyperventilating. I can't believe I let myself lose control like that. I know for a fact that I didn't want Lisa, Monica, whatever her damn name is anymore, but my body wasn't listening to my brain.

Lisa sensed the same thing, and began to chuckle stepping in closer to me.

"Baby, why are you fighting this?" She tried to move in closer to me, but I went behind my desk. I had a silent alarm underneath it, and was ready to press the button.

Quickly, Lisa pulled her dress up over her head, and dropped it to the floor. Seductively, she climbed onto of my desk and undid her bra. "Baby, we are supposed to be together, you don't miss me?"

Avoiding her actions and questions all together, I darted toward the door, and grabbed my items off the ground.

"Lisa, I am only going to tell you this once. Stay the hell away from me, my business and my family. You are NOT my wife!" I opened my office door, and rushed out. "I am going to call the police if you are not out of here in ten minutes."

Not even waiting for a response, I made a dash for the elevator. Once I was inside and the door was closing was when I finally turned my attention back to my office door. Only in her panties, Lisa was standing inside the door frame, with tears in her eyes. As the door closed, the hairs on my neck stood to attention again as I watched a sadistic smile form across her lips.

From the Pen of *Nicola*

Somebody's Watching

Me

Gabrielle

"Baby, when are you coming to bed?" seductively I asked while massaging his neck. Anthony was alone in his study finishing up some work. The baby was asleep and I was horny. I wanted his attention entirely on me. Since we had AJ, we rarely got moments alone. Daphne, our maid, helped out a lot, but I wanted to make sure that my son knew that I was his mother. Therefore, I made sure I spent quality time with AJ, which left little time for us, unless he was sleep or with Daphne.

"Un momento chicka," Anthony purred to me kissing each one of my finger tips.

A loud moan escaped my throat as I leaned in closer to my man. I wanted him to make love to me so badly, that I could feel myself begin to cream in between my legs. Anthony knew I needed some special attention, but was trying to make me beg for it. Slowly, I ran my tongue down the edge of his ear lobe.

"Mommy..." I am not going to be able to finish this if you don't stop it." He chuckled batting away my hands. I knew for a fact that it was hard for my husband to say no to me, when I was in this type of mood. Slowly, he pulled me down onto his lap and kissed me tenderly on the lips.

This was the moment I was waiting for. I needed some affection, patience and understanding from my husband. Anthony was totally different from the other men that I had in the past. He was a dream come true, and damn did I believe in him. I believed that he was a great provider, an ideal father, a wonderful husband and the absolute best friend that I have ever had.

Anthony ran his fingers through my hair as he parted my lips with his tongue and rummaged my mouth. He whispered sweet nothings in between kisses which made chills run through my body, shivering down my spine. Damn, I can't control myself. I wanted this man so bad. I loved his every touch and the very sound of his voice. My sun rose and set to this man and he knew it.

Raising the thin cloth of my t-shirt, Anthony gathered my small breast within his palms and played with my nipples. I threw my head back in excitement craving for his touch. My heart was beating rapidly, my breath running wild, and the feeling that I was feeling inside was priceless. I didn't want it to end.

Once the warmth of his tongue reached my quarter shaped nipples, I gasped. My kitty was quivering, longing to feel him deep inside of me. "Baby, I love you," I whispered grabbing the back of his head. I held his head in place not wanting him to stop. The touching and teasing that he was doing with his tongue and hands were driving me crazy. I wanted him to hear the melodies that my body was singing to him and feel the excitement that was pouring out of me. I was at a point of no return, and the only thing I needed was for him to make love to me like never before.

Gracefully picking me up, Anthony carried me over to our king-sized bed, tenderly laying me down. His lips expressed such a sweet smile as he removed my t-shirt and panties. Slowly he parted my legs, massaging my inner thighs and calves muscles.

"Please taste me, please...." I begged, biting down on my lower lip. Maintaining his smooth debonair smile, Anthony made it clear that he was enjoying every moment of this seduction that he was putting on me. He took his time as he descended downwards toward my dripping sweet nectar. The moment of impact was breath taking as the small of my back curved and my body continued to shudder.

My sexy husband took his time as he made love to me with his mouth. I could no longer control myself and I moaned out loud, calling his name over and over again.

"Baby... you taste so sweet. You like what Daddy is doing to you don't you?"

Anthony continued his perfect performance, never letting up on me. If he wasn't using his mouth, he was penetrating me with his fingers. I came so much that I lost count. Not thinking that I could take anymore, I begged him to stop as he held onto my clit for dear life. At the point that I thought that I couldn't take anymore is when I heard my door knob turn.

My body froze as I grabbed Anthony's shoulders. Even though the servants lived onsite, they lived in a separate area. No one should have been in our wing besides AJ who resided in the bedroom next to ours.

"Baby! Someone is coming in! Oh my goodness, cover us up. It took me a moment to break the mojo that my baby had going, but once he realized what I was saying, he did the exact opposite from my request.

The hairs on the back of my neck stood straight up because I felt as if someone was watching me. "Anthony! Stop it and get up! Somebody is outside our door. Can you be the *man* and find out what is going on please!" I fussed at him.

Not believing that I was pushing him off of me, Anthony positioned himself on his hands and knees straddled above me, clearly annoyed. "What are you talking about? NO one is coming in here. You are hearing things, but if it is bothering you like that, *let me be a man* and check for you."

Anthony stood up, fixing his pajama bottoms mumbling under his breath to himself. It wasn't until he turned around in the direction of our bedroom door and saw that it was cracked ajar that he understood my concern.

'What the hell?" Anthony said to no one in particular. He knew just like I did that I closed that door behind me when I entered.

"Stay right there, I will be right back," he told me as he quietly opened the door.

I have been living in fear ever since the day that I went into labor and Monique was killed. I knew for a fact that I seen Lisa staring at me as I got into the ambulance but everyone has been trying to convince me that I was seeing things.

"How would she have known that we were in Los Angeles?" Andrice has told me on several occasions. I knew that I wasn't crazy. I knew who she was. I have stood and stared at this lady outside the window of my office when I used to be Anthony's assistant. She would stay outside for hours pacing the sidewalk in hopes of an opportunity to speak to him. So I knew exactly what she looked like.

Lisa was beautiful. She was of average height, possessed an athletic physique, and the shiniest blonde hair that I have ever seen. At the time, it was apparent that she was taking their separation to heart, but her beauty is what always stuck out to me. The only difference between the Lisa that I remembered and the one I seen in Los Angeles was the hair color. The lady in LA wore a page boy hair cut, brown in color.

During the divorce, Anthony and I were just starting to get to know each other and become friends, so he kept me and that situation totally opposite. The only thing that I knew for a fact was that she was crazy, and

Anthony was trying to get the hell away from her.

Now here we were, two years later, and I was scared to death of this woman. Paranoid, I am constantly looking over my shoulder, second guessing every step I took and move that I made. I tried to keep my fears to myself because I didn't want Anthony to leave me the way he left Lisa. My husband had a low tolerance for bull shit and I tried my best to not give him any. At what point does one's fears turn into obsession and nagging? I didn't want to be that complaining angry woman, but my paranoia was getting the best of me. I was suspect of any and every thing. Nervously, I grabbed my cell off of the night stand, and clutched it to my breast, waiting for Anthony to return.

From the Pen of *Nicola*

Let me Work on That

Andrice

It has only been a month since Carmello decided that he needed help raising Monique's girls, and brought them back to Jersey to stay with Loretta. Everyone thought it would be best for the girls to be with their brothers and the rest of their support system. We all have been trying to help as much as we can with the girls to make them feel loved. It was already bad enough that they had to lose their mother, but to have the only father figure that they have had for a while, abandon them as well, has destroyed them.

Earlier that day we all went to watch Michael and Robert run up and down the soccer field participating in an amazing game. The boys were going to have a celebration dinner with their team at Dave & Busters, so I offered to take the girls with me so that Loretta could go home and get some rest. Gabby and AJ rode with me to the game since Anthony left this morning for Maryland. His mother's house finally had an offer, damn near two years later after her death, and since Gabrielle has been going through so much lately, he felt as if it was best for her to stay at home.

I unlocked the doors to my Denali, and informed the girls to go all the way to third row of seats.

"Mami, I still don't see why you have such a big ole' truck for only one person, but hey, it sure is coming in handy for us today, so I really can't complain." Gabrielle said laughing buckling AJ into his car seat.

A Cold Piece

To hear her laugh was so pleasant, and I had to admit I missed it. I am always the voice of reason, ensuring everyone that everything will be okay, but damn this was such a hard role to fill. I was getting tired of being everyone's super hero, everyone except Gabrielle. I loved this girl so much. I watched her securing her son and at the same time, making sure that Justice and Lyric were also secure. She made such an excellent mother. The fears that she has been experiencing lately were hindering her from her motherly role, and I have been trying to figure out a way for her to get back on track.

I could see it all in her face as I watched her get out of her black five series Mercedes. The guard at the gate informed me that she was here, so I decided to meet her in the parking garage instead of making her lug AJ and all his baby necessities upstairs to my condo. Her typical happy demeanor was shadowed by sadness. She reminded me of Eyore, from the Hundred Acre Woods. I decided I was going to be a combination of Christopher Robin and Winnie the Pooh. I was going to put a smile on her face, while coming to the root of whatever it was that was bothering her.

Quickly I rushed over and hugged my friend. I removed AJ from the car, car seat and all, and asked her to punch in the code to unlock my doors. Even though I do not have any children of my own, I was able to get him buckled up and secured in no time. Moments later we were all buckled in and about to head to the game.

"Hold on Mama, let me get out and lock my door. My batteries are going dead or something on my alarm because it takes forever to lock and unlock my door." Gabrielle hopped out the truck and went over to the car and manually locked the doors.

"Anthony was trying to change the batteries before he left, but we didn't have any lying around the house," she informed me while settling back into the seat. "He told me to be ghetto and bang the remote against something, but that trick just didn't work for me when I tried."

I chuckled at the thought of her banging on the remote.

"Don't laugh at me heifa," Gabby told me playfully tapping me on the arm. "Girl, I really needed that laugh. There has been so much going on that I think I forgot how to laugh. I just want my life back, I just don't know what to do to get it back on track, but I need to do something, like now girl."

This shit was starting to take a toll on her for real as I listened to her on the ride to the game, telling me of several different occasions that it felt as if someone was watching her. She has had this feeling while she was out and about, but the encounters in which she was at home gave me the creeps and shot chills throughout my entire body.

She told me how hard it was for her and Anthony to make love ever since the baby's arrival, and she had finally found an opportunity to have some alone time. In the middle of their "session", Gabby heard her bedroom door open and made Anthony go investigate. They didn't find anyone in the house, but AJ's car seat was lying on the floor in front of his crib instead of inside the closet. Anthony tried to convince her that she must have left it there by accident, but Gabby said that she was positive that she left the seat in the closet.

"Someone has been in my house Andrice! I know it. I told Anthony, that I needed him to get security cameras installed soon, or me and my son were moving in with my Father." Gabrielle placed her face inside of her trembling hands and cried out. "I don't know what to do Dricie... I think I am going crazy."

I pulled over and consoled her, promising her that everything was going to be okay. I made a mental note to myself that I needed to speak to Anthony directly and get the entire story about this Lisa chick, and if he felt that she was really behind Mo's accident, and is now stalking Gabby.

Once we got to the game I observed Gabby and noticed that her spirits were brighter, which was a good thing. Once we got back to the vehicle, I started the engine and adjusted my radio station to something that I knew the girls would enjoy listening to, 88.1, as Gabby finally got settled into the passenger seat and secured her own belt. "Thank you girl for clearing my mind today, I needed this quality time."

I smiled at my friend and squeezed her hand. "It is going to be okay girl," I reassured her. "You need a vacation away from everything. Let me work on that for you... I got you." Turning my attention to the girls, I asked, "Where do you ladies want to go for dinner?"

I waited for the girls to respond, but instead I got silence. I adjusted my rear view mirror, and seen that they were knocked out cuddled up to each other. Just like the rest of us, they were taking the loss of their mother to heart and haven't been the same since the incident. Today was the first time that I have seen them smile as well, so maybe it was destined for all of us to be together today.

"Girl, they are asl--," I started to tell Gabrielle, but was stopped mid sentence. She was fast asleep too with her head resting against the window. Taking in a deep breath, I continued my journey home. While driving I decided that I was going to just order a couple of pizzas and chicken wings from Pizza Hut, and have everyone stay the night.

Smiling to myself, I pulled up to the guard house, and waved at Edgar, the security guard. Smiling back, he waved as well and buzzed us into the gate. I went down to the bottom level of the parking garage, and pulled into my spot. Everyone was still sound asleep, so I decided to help Gabby out and put AJ's stroller back into her car so she would not have to do it later.

Quietly, I rummaged through her purse and pulled out her keys. I hopped out of my truck and opened the rear door. Struggling, I pulled the stroller out of and held it upright to close the door back. *Damn, how the hell is her little ass doing this by herself?* I thought to myself. I carried the stroller over to her car and pushed the trunk button on her remote. No lights clicked on, and I didn't hear the trunk pop.

"Oh shit," I said under my breath. I forgot I had to bang on it. Laughing out loud I tapped the remote against the trunk a couple of times. I pushed the open trunk button again, but I wasn't prepared for what happened next. I heard the trunk pop but I also heard a beep. I looked down to see if it was my cell phone that I usually wore on my hip, but this time it was sitting inside my cup holder.

I opened the trunk and struggled to place the stroller inside. The beeping sound rang out two more times followed by a loud crash. Before I could move a burst of fire exploded from her car, shooting me across the parking lot as if I was as light as a bird's feather. I heard a ringing in my ears and then everything around me went black.

Never Prepared

Anthony

My brother pushed the papers across the table for me to sign. It was official; a young Nigerian couple just purchased my mother's house. It has been almost two years since the day her staff found her floating in her bath tub. The Medical Examiner informed us that she had been dead for at least six hours before anyone found her.

Who prepares a child to bury their mother? That was the hardest thing for me to do in my life. My mother was my best friend, and I have been missing her terribly since she has been gone. She was prepared for the worst and had everything set in detail in regards to how she wanted to be buried. Everything was picked out and paid for, which made me uneasy.

Malcolm and I were the only ones that had to be there to sign off on the property because she left us the estate. At first we were going to keep it because no one wanted to really believe that she was gone. Everything was the exact way that she left it, even down to her hair brush that still housed strands of her fine gray hair.

The first couple of months after her death past like a blur. I damn near moved into her house just so I could walk the halls and smell her scent. Her presence in the home is distinctively there, and I wanted to be as close to her as possible. After the first year passed by though, her scent no longer lingered in the air. The only scent that could be detected now was dust and mold. It was a painful decision, but we decided that it was going to be for the best if we sold it. The house was only on the market for eight weeks before someone made an offer. Neither one of us wanted to drag the process out, so we quickly agreed to the low offer that the couple put on the table.

We spent the duration of the day guiding the movers as they packed up the second level of the house and moved them out. At first we were just going to give everything away to a charity for underprivileged families, but none of us had the stomach for it. We quickly agreed to just have everything moved into a storage unit until we were comfortable with giving her items, part of her history, away.

Now almost twelve hours later, we sat alone in the house having to take care of the inevitable. Sighing deeply, I looked over the paper work and signed my John Hancock on the bottom of the document. Tears were in the corners of my eyes, as I looked around the room again.

"Malcolm, did it ever cross your mind of what really happened to Mama?" I asked my brother staring at the ceiling. "So many crazy events have been going on in my world that it has me questioning everything crazy that has happened to me and the people around me."

My brother listened as I poured my heart out about everything that has been going on. Out of my entire family, just Malcolm and my mother were the only ones that I entrusted the whole truth about Lisa. He was the one that suggested for me not to get the authorities involved and just separate myself completely without her knowing. At the time, we both agreed that setting up another residence and then cutting her off completely would be the best route for everyone involved, but now I am not too sure.

After I finished explaining everything from Monique's death, to Lisa popping up at my office, and now how Gabrielle is convinced that someone is following her, my brother's eyes widened.

104

"So you think that your ex-wife Lisa has something to do with all of this, Mother included?" he asked rubbing his chin.

Silently nodding yes, my mind began to wonder. The logical side of me wanted to believe that this was all just a coincidence, but I had to face the obvious and be honest with myself. There was too much going on around me to just think that. Then when she showed up at my job, like we haven't been divorced for two years? You do not have to be a rocket scientist to figure this one out.

Before I could respond, my cell phone rang, scaring the shit out of both of us. I walked over to the couch and checked the caller id. It was Gabrielle.

"Hey baby girl, how goes it?" I asked smiling as I spoke. I needed to hear her voice right now to let me know that everything is okay. She was my rock, and if I didn't have her, I don't know where the hell I would be right now.

"Anthony! She is going to kill me! Dricie may die! My car exploded. Anthony! What did I do? Why is she after me?" my wife sobbed into the phone.

"WHAT! Your car exploded? Where are you? What happened to Andrice? Calm down baby and tell me what happened." Cupping the mouth piece of the blackberry, I turned my attention to my brother and told him to book us a flight back to Jersey right now.

Gabrielle continued to cry not saying a word. I grabbed my keys off of the table and my sports coat. Malcolm was right behind me securing the house. I tried to soothe her so that she could tell me what happened, but my words were not working. The next thing I knew, the line went dead.

Starting the car, I struggled dialing her number back. It only rang twice before a child answered.

"Uncle Anthony? Is this you?" a soft voice asked me crying as well.

"Yes it is. Who is this?" I asked wondering who I was talking too.

"It's Lyric, Uncle. Auntie is not doing good. The paramedics took her to the side to give her some oxygen. Are you on your way? They are taking Ti Ti Andi to the hospital. She won't wake up Uncle. Her face and body is all burned up. I hope she doesn't die like Mommy did."

I was trying to take in everything that she just said. This was too much for any adult to take on, let alone a child that just lost her own mother.

"Lyric, yes I am on my way," I assured her in a calm voice. "Where are you? Where is the baby? How did Auntie's car blow up? Is your sister okay?" I had so many questions, but I needed her to answer me and let me know that my family is okay. If Lisa is behind this, then I am going to have put a stop to this and quick. I can't jeopardize anyone else's safety, do to me being selfish.

"Yes sir, me, AJ, and Justice are okay. We were asleep in Ti Ti's truck coming back from our brother's game. The next thing I knew I heard a crash, and opened my eyes to see Ti Ti Andi and the stroller fly in the air. We are at her house. Please Uncle, hurry and come. We need you. There are a lot of police cars, fire trucks and ambulances here."

I reassured her that I was on my way, and told her to have Gabrielle call me as soon as the EMT was finished with her. I dropped my phone into my lap as tears spilled down my cheeks. My brother patted me on the back, but didn't say a word. He finished making our flight arrangements and turned his attention to the window. We rode in silence the rest of the way to the airport.

Unfortunate Circumstances

Lisa

Sitting down at my kitchen table with a bowl of grape nut flakes and a banana, I turned my attention to the small television that flipped down out of the cabinets. A breaking news report was coming on, about a car explosion that happened last night. The reporter told about a woman, mid thirties, who was in intensive care on life support after a car explosion in an exclusive Alpine, New Jersey community parking garage.

Garage? They do not have a parking garage? I listened in detail as the reporter explained that it was a black 2011 5 series Mercedes that was involved in the explosion. My heart skipped a beat as I tried to scan the scene and see if I recognized the location, but I didn't see anything.

Hmm. I wonder if that was her. Picking up my remote I began switching channels to see if the explosion was covered by any other stations. All the major networks were covering the story, but were giving out limited information. I guess the only way I was going to find out is if I researched myself, and go back to the house.

A smile crept up the corners of my mouth as I thought about the last time I was inside of the *fake* Oliver's household. My initial plan was to take the baby, but I heard the happy couple giggling and moaning so I had to investigate. My plan was to open the door and peek in, but the door knob squeaked as I turned it to the left. I heard Gabrielle gasp and I took a couple of steps back, holding my breath as I listened to the pair.

A Cold Piece

I have had so many nightmares of them having sex. He would make love to her the same way that he used to make love to me. Squeezing her breast, slapping her ass and talking dirty too her. The thought of him penetrating her would always send chills running up and down my spine and I would wake u in a cold sweat. I could hear the beating of my heart in my ears and throughout my body. I would always have to rock myself with my arms crossed telling myself to get it together.

Shit! Gabrielle heard the door knob. She was whispering frantically that someone was out there. Part of me wanted to go in there and choke her whining ass until she passed out, but if I was going to execute my plan, I needed to hurry and go into the baby's room and leave the love birds alone. I needed for the *new* Mrs. Oliver to hurt as badly as she has made me hurt and even though choking her to death, would make me temporarily feel better, it would be just too easy.

Quietly, I hurried into AJ's room, and stood over the sleeping body. I have watched him many nights infatuated at the fact of how much he looked like his father. I have even rocked him back to sleep the nights that he fussed and craved for attention. He was such a beautiful baby. It wasn't going to be hard to pass him as my own child. I was either going to have him all to myself, or as a family with Anthony. It was his choice.

I went into the closet and picked up the car seat. I was almost at the crib when I heard Gabrielle yell out at Anthony. I laid the car seat down and hurried into the closet, like a thief in the night. I couldn't let them catch me in their house, so I pulled out the small hand revolver I had tucked into my pants and waited. The door to AJ's room opened and I heard heavy footsteps.

"What is this doing here?" I heard him say quietly. My heart was pounding and the hairs on the back of my neck stood straight up. I didn't want to shoot my man, but I would if he came after me.

I could hear him say some soft words to the baby. I needed to see what he was doing, so I positioned myself to see out the small crack of the closet opening. Damn, Anthony still sexy as ever was wearing only a pair of pajama pants, showing his muscular back and chest, I just wanted to fuck him right then and there. But I had to keep my composure and calm myself. He picked up his son and kissed him on the forehead. The sight was so beautiful. I didn't know that I was crying until I felt the tears rolling down my cheeks.

It was at that moment that I decided that I was not going to take the baby away from him; I was just going to have to make Gabrielle go away.

Leaving the room, Anthony took the baby into their bedroom. It wasn't until I heard their bedroom door shut completely, that I scurried out of the closet, and out of their house. I didn't look back, until I was safely inside my own car.

I sat alone in the dark watching their house. I stayed there until the sun rose behind me. I watched the servants get up, and then forty-five minutes later seen Anthony leave. I waited until I seen the tail lights of his truck disappear, and then I started my car and slowly drove past the house. While I was out there I came up with a plan A and plan B. If plan A didn't work, then I would have to really implement plan B.

Three weeks later, I am here sitting in my house watching the news trying to see if plan A worked. I had hired Jared, an old friend of mine in Minnesota to create a car alarm bomb for me. When I met him, he was a half way loony ex marine that worked as a weapons expert. He just needed attention, and didn't mind paying you for it.

A Cold Piece

Since I was *still* Mrs. Oliver, I went down to Planet Mercedes dealership and informed them that I needed another alarm for my vehicle and my key cut. It took ten days for the pieces to come, but the time was well worth the wait.

While lying in my bed, I watched him create the igniter for the bomb with the memory board. Once he was done, he went over the particulars of how and where I need to place the actual bomb. I listened intensively as he rambled off the instructions. Everything seemed simple enough, so I took him on for the challenge.

I paid Anthony and Gabrielle another late night visit, this time only for a moment. I switched out the alarms, and used my key to place the bomb under the driver's seat. It felt like an eternity for this day to come. I needed to be sure that it was Gabrielle though. I needed that reassurance.

I finished my cereal and rinsed out my bowl. I went over to my cookie jar and pulled out the only item that it housed. I was going to call Gabrielle.

Somebody Pray for Me

Loretta

"Gabby, did she wake up yet?" I asked, clutching my cell phone close to my ear. I was coming down Central Avenue, almost to East Orange Hospital. This was my fifth time calling, and each time I have gotten the same response.

"No Mami, she hasn't. Are you almost here? I want to rest my eyes for a moment, but I don't want to leave the girls responsible for AJ. Anthony should be here soon. I don't know why I feel so tired. I think the EMT workers gave me something to put me to sleep."

"Okay baby girl, I am almost there. I am about a block away. Is there anything that I can get for you before I get there?" I asked. After the boys' game, I was exhausted but felt very fatigued. I took a Tylenol pm so that I could sleep peacefully. I was sleeping so peacefully that I didn't hear the twenty-eight missed calls from the girls and Gabrielle.

It wasn't until the boys came home and told me that Auntie was on the house phone; that is when I really woke up. It has been a long time since I was able to sleep for a couple of hours straight, and my body didn't know how to react to it. I continued to lay in the bed with my eyes closed barely holding the receiver.

"Hello," I whispered into the phone.

I could barely make out Gabrielle's voice through her sobs, but I did understand the most important. Andrice was in the hospital from third degree burns. I sat up in the bed, and tried to calm her down. What did she mean that Andrice has been burned, and where were the girls? Ever since Mello gave them too me, I have been feeling very overprotective. Michael hasn't had anything to do with the boys or the girls since Monique and I became friends, so who really did they have besides me?

Those girls have been through so much, that while I was concerned about the well being of Dricie, I needed to make sure that the two of them were okay too. Once reassured, I put back on my clothes, had the boys pile into the car, and rushed over to the hospital.

I pulled into the parking lot and quickly found a place to park. My heart was pounding in my chest as I instructed the boys to hurry and get out of the car. Once inside, we followed the directions to the Intensive Care Burn Unit.

119

The entire ride over, I was going back and forth with everything that has happened as well as all the crap that Gabrielle has told me. When they first got married, I told Gabrielle maybe it wasn't a good idea since he recently divorced his wife because, according to him, "she was crazy." It sounded like a typical excuse that most men have for their ex, and I tried to warn her that once he gets tired of her, she was going to be the crazy bitch too. Monique and I had both been down this road with our donor, so I was trying to prepare her for the worst. At the time, I was convinced that the worst would be a string of women, him possibly cheating on her with his *new* assistant, or him being too busy with work to enjoy her and their family. I am now a believer that the ex is really crazy.

Once we reached the burn unit, I spotted Justice, Lyric, and AJ alone in the waiting room. There were two police officers standing guard outside the door. I had to show the officer's my identification before they would let me into the room.

The girls were curled up together with AJ's tiny body tucked between them. It was a precious sight during a terrible situation. I bent down next to the couch and kissed all three of them on the forehead. All of their eyes remained shut not even stirring at the gesture. Gabrielle was claiming exhaustion, but by their action, so were the kids.

"Boys sit down next to your sister's and wait for me to come back. I am going to check on Auntie and Ti Ti Andi okay?" My babies nodded yes in unison, and turned their attention to Shake it Up on the television perched in the corner.

I was about to ask the charge nurse to direct me to the room of Andrice Bennett but quickly figured out the way. There were two more officers outside her door. I hurried down the corridor, pulling my id back out. Once they looked it over and checked to see if my name was on their list, I was finally able to step inside. The room was dark and I could hear the machines beeping from outside the door. Quietly I opened the door and entered the room. Gabrielle was asleep sitting up in a chair posted next to the bed.

Gently I tapped her on the shoulder startling her. She jumped up, uncrossing her arms and looked up at me. "Hey girl, it's you," Gabrielle mumbled standing up to give me a hug. "I can't believe I fell asleep. Oh my goodness, my back is killing me."

I flashed a weak smile and turned my attention to Andrice wrapped up in the bed. I wasn't prepared to see her like that. She appeared swollen underneath all of the bandages. The only thing that wasn't wrapped was her eyes, small holes allowing her to breathe and her lips.

Turning my attention back to Gabrielle, meekly I asked, "What is going to happen to her?"

Tears swelled up in Gabrielle's eyes as she informed me of Dricie's status. "She has third degree burns throughout her body, but she is stable. It is going to be a long road to recovery for her, but the doctor believes she will pull through this."

"Of course she is going to pull through, she got us to take care of her," I chuckled trying to lighten up the situation. "How long before her parents get here from Long Island?" I asked.

"They are on their way," she said stretching her arms over her head. The look in Gabrielle's eyes was making me uncomfortable. I have not seen her like this, ever. She has always been the cool, optimistic one out of our crew, but since the loss of Mo, she has been so different.

"Honey, go out there and lay with the babies. I will sit here with Andi okay?" I stepped in to give Gabrielle a hug holding her extra tight. I knew that she blamed herself for what happened. It was not her fault at all. What really was making me scared to death is the thought that the bomb was set for her.

"They are going to find whoever did this, I promise you," I reassured her rubbing her back. I tried to remain calm and not allow her to see me cry. After a few more moments, Gabrielle finally broke our embrace and left the room to join the kids.

I took her place in the chair and ran my finger tip over Andi's left hand. The moment I did, I heard a moan come from Andrice.

"Hey lady, I am here to take care of you," I said to her standing back up.

"Some, Some, Somebody... P, P, P, Pray for me," Andrice struggled to get out. The tears that I kept bottled up trying to be strong, finally escaped and broke free.

"Of course sweetie, of course," I told her continuing to rub her hand.

Father God,

We come to you with sincere hearts. May you please watch over Andrice, and guide her quickly down a road to recovery. Please God, heal her and bless her. We all thank you Lord, for sparing her life, but will you please take care of her Lord. And God, wrap your arms of peace around Gabrielle. Someone is after her Lord, and it is damaging all of us in the process. Please save us Lord. We all need you right now. In the name of Jesus we pray.... Amen.

From the Pen of *Nicola*

126

Get the Authorities Involved

Gabrielle

It felt like an eternity for Anthony to finally get here. Andrice has been through two surgeries already, and her family just arrived from New York. I felt so helpless and distraught. Loretta and the kids were still here with me, as we all made our selves at home in the waiting room.

Officers were in and out, asking us what felt like the same questions over and over again, trying to figure out what exactly took place. What was left of my car was being impounded by the police for forensic observation. Once it was known that I am the wife of THE Anthony Oliver, it seemed to have given them some pep in their step. Anthony and the Oliver family were well known throughout the east coast, especially since his headquarters was right here in Jersey. The police chief was the one giving me updates personally, and informed me that once my husband's plane touched down, that there would be a police escort waiting for him at the airport.

There was so much hustle and bustle going on around me that it was any wonder that any of us were able to get some rest, let alone falling asleep; but we did. Loretta and I took turns watching over Andrice, until we were informed that her parents were here. We both agreed that they needed that private time with her to reassure her everything was going to be okay.

A Cold Piece

Anthony. Anthony. Anthony.

Even though I loved this man to death, I was starting to feel the biggest amount of resentment for him. I told him from day one that I knew Lisa was behind this and that we needed to get the police involved, but he insisted that I was just upset. He said that we didn't have any proof that it was Lisa, and that we could not just go around blaming her for everything bad that has happened in our lives. I was shocked the first time he told me this three days after the birth of AJ. This was coming from the same man that left her and damn near vanished without a trace. I didn't know the entire story behind Lisa, but I promise you, before I lose another love one, I was going to find out.

I blamed myself for everything that has happened to my friends up until this point. If it wasn't for my relationship with my husband, everyone would still be here unharmed. Just knowing that the car bomb was actually intended for me just sickened me. What if I did what Anthony told me, and made the remote work? What if I was trying to put my son into his car seat and the bomb went off? AJ's precious body would not have been able to withstand that type of explosion.

I know how selfish this sounds, but I don't know what I would do if that was me laying in the bed, and AJ was taken from me. I think I would have willed myself to just die. Before AJ came into my life, I never knew I could feel this type of love for anyone in the world, but now I don't know what I would do if I did not have him here to share my world. Yes, I loved my husband, and my father, but the love that I am experiencing for my child is the type of love that I never knew I could have in my life.

Feeling a gentle kiss on my forehead is what made me realize that I had fallen asleep. I forced my eyes open to be greeted by a smile from Anthony.

"Hey baby," was the simple sentence that he spoke.

I don't know how long I was asleep for, but I did doze off with AJ cuddled up to my bosom. Anthony removed the baby from my arms and held him close to his chest. It wasn't until I heard the voice behind him that I realized he wasn't alone.

"How are you doing Sis?" Malcolm's voice spoke softly from behind Anthony.

Pushing myself up into a sitting position, I motioned for him to come over and give me a hug. It has been awhile since I seen my brother in-law, and I knew he needed this hug just as much as I did. I knew for a fact that Anthony and Malcolm were the closest of the four brothers, and they were Mother Elizabeth's pride and joy.

Wait a minute! Mother Elizabeth! I wonder if this bitch had something to do with her death?!? That is something else that I am going to have to look into. I still had Michael, the private investigator's contact information in my old rolodex. I remember coming across his name while we were in the process of transferring Anthony's contact list into a digital filing system. I quickly copied the number down and stuck it into my rolodex. At the time, Anthony and I were just becoming close, so I didn't know that two years later, we were going to be together. I did know I didn't want to go through what he did and was going to have a background check ran on the person that I was going to spend the rest of my life with.

Malcolm sat down in the wooden chair close to the television, while I made room for Anthony to sit down where my feet were. Loretta was fast asleep on the opposite sofa, while both set of the twins were snuggled together on a makeshift pallet that the nursing staff created for them. I told Lo, that she should take the children home, but she shook her head no, and informed me that she was not going anywhere.

"I called Daphne and told her to come up here and get the baby," Anthony told me while laying my head on his lap. He needs a bath, and to change into some clean clothes. Also, it is not good for him to be up here with all these germs floating all around."

I was about to object when my cell phone rang. I reached over to the coffee table and was about to answer it, but before even looking at the caller id, I gave it to Anthony. Everyone that I needed to speak to knew what was going on, so anyone else was just irrelevant.

"Hello," Anthony spoke into the receiver. "Hello?"

Anthony had a puzzled look on his face, as he repeated his salutations over and over into the phone. He looked at the caller ID, and then placed the phone back to his ear.

"Lisa? Is that you?" he asked with a look of panic on his face. Pushing me up out of his lap and handing me the baby, Anthony stepped outside the waiting room, with Malcolm quickly behind him. Clutching my son close, my heart began to pound. I watched them outside the window speaking to the officers that continued to stand guard. I didn't know what they were saying, but I did know what I was thinking. Finally, it was okay for the police to be involved.

Why is she calling my phone? How the hell she get my number? Not once throughout this entire ordeal has this chick tried to contact me, but ironically the same day my car blows up, she is on my phone.

I rocked back and forth on the sofa, nodding my head.

"She is going to kill me." I repeatedly whispered to myself.

A Cold Piece

I felt like all of my life was draining out of my body as I waited for Anthony to come back in.

Twelve Weeks Later

Taking Losses

Anthony

"Okay baby, tell Andrice, I said Hey and that I am proud of her, call me when you are on your way home," I informed my wife.

AJ and I were relaxing in bed, watching some Saturday late morning football. Gabrielle left early to visit Andrice at the rehabilitation center. When I say that I am proud of her, I really do mean it. She has come such a long way over the last couple of weeks, longer than I think I would in her situation.

She was now starting to say more sentences and sip through a straw. Even though that seems like nothing to the average person, for someone who suffers from second and third degree burns over more than seventy five percent of their body, was a miracle.

So much has happened since the explosion. I was trying to think of what I could do special for Gabrielle to give her as a token of my love and appreciation. She was scared for her life, and I kept pushing it to the side as if she was tripping. I should have protected my family better. That bomb was intended for my wife, and it wasn't until I almost lost her and my son that I manned up and really put in an effort to protect them.

I now have an alarm system installed with hidden cameras placed throughout my home. I wasn't going to be taking any more losses when it came to my family if I could help it.

After all of my wife's pain and suffering, I think that she deserved the 2012 Bentley Geneva that I purchased for her which included a top-of-the-line tracking device as well. Even though Gabrielle was happy and thankful of the added security, she was still living on edge.

It wasn't until the detective gave us a follow-up two weeks ago on their investigation of Lisa. That is when she finally started to relax and breathe a little. Detective Harris came by claiming that she had good news and bad news, asking us which one we wanted her to start off with. We invited her into our family room, and asked Daphne to come and get the baby.

Once we were all settled, she started her story. "The bad news is... Lisa has not been arrested. We do have a warrant out for her arrest, and we have contacted the Minnesota authorities letting them know of the alias that she has been living under for the last several years, but when we went to arrest her, she was gone."

"Gone, what do you mean gone?" Gabrielle asked barely over a whisper I had the same question, but the words slipped out of her mouth first.

"Well let me tell you the good news, and then I can explain in detail what I mean by her being gone," Detective Harris interjected. "You see, when you informed the officer at the hospital of everything that had happened, we didn't have any probable cause connecting her to all of the events that you told us about. I mean it was good that she called your phone Mrs. Oliver, but in actuality, any good lawyer could get that thrown out. Under the direct orders of the Police Chief, is how we even got any evidence placing Lisa, I mean Monica, in the same vicinity for these crimes.

We have footage of her stopping for gas a block away from your home, the same day that you said you felt someone was in the house. So that, included with the phone call, is what got us a search warrant for her home. Once inside we hit the jackpot. We found individual photos of the two of you, your home, your car and even your son inside of his crib."

Gabrielle gasped but didn't interrupt.

"There was a receipt from a local car dealership for Mrs. Oliver; it was for the key and alarm for the same make and model of your vehicle that was blown up. There was even a check list of things to do, including "visit my husband" that went along with the story that you told us Mr. Oliver of when she came to your office trying to seduce you."

The trance that Gabrielle was in was broken the moment the officer spoke about her coming to the office. She glanced back and forth between the two of us, but still didn't say a word. The look on her face told it all.

"So, like I said the bad news is that she hasn't been caught yet, but the good news is that we have several agencies looking for her, so this chapter of your life should be closed sooner than later."

"Well, thank you ma'am for all of your help". Gabrielle said to no one in particular while standing up. "I am glad that you people are all over it. Keep us posted if you find out anything else. "

Gabrielle then got up and left the room.

"Is everything okay with her?" The Detective asked me puzzled by Gabby's abrupt departure. "I know that she been through a lot."

"Yes, she is okay." I informed her, already understanding why Gabrielle was upset. "She is just tired."

I finished listening to her go over what else the police department was in the process of doing to apprehend Lisa, and finally she left. I went upstairs to find Gabrielle and explain to her why I didn't tell her about my unexpected visit from Lisa, but she was fast asleep with my son cradled in her arms.

A Cold Piece

I have to admit. After speaking to Detective Harris, I am truly scared to death. If I had just gone with my first mind, and had Lisa arrested, the New Jersey Police Department would not be on a quest to find her. I hope that she is back in Minnesota or wherever the hell she is from.

Things were so different in my house; I feel like I am losing my wife. Every time I try to bring it up to her, she informs me that she doesn't want to talk about it. She has been walking around in a daze, and at times it was making me feel uncomfortable. Thankfully, the look of fear that she had possessed for so long has finally went away. Now it was my time to try to fix my marriage with my wife. Hopefully the upcoming holiday season will fix our troubled home.

From the Pen of *Nicola*

Finally, the Truth

Gabrielle

Quietly, I opened the door to my bedroom trying not to wake my husband. I told Anthony that I was going out to a Pre-Thanksgiving event with Loretta. He didn't object and was somewhat happy that I was finally getting out and doing it on my own.

Softly, I closed the door behind me, and placed my keys and cell phone on the dresser.

The sound of Cold Train could be heard from the Bose surround sound system in our bedroom. One by one, I removed my gold

Prada heels, and unzipped my dress, letting it drop down around my feet.

My emotions were all over the place. I did go to a bar with Loretta, but it wasn't for any holiday celebration. We went there to meet up with Michael, Anthony's private investigator. A bar was an adequate location to meet up with him; because I indeed needed a drink after learning all that I did tonight.

Ever since Andrice's accident, I have been so distant from my husband. The information about Lisa scared the shit out of me but finding out all that my husband had done to protect me, made me look at him in a whole different light. I was starting to doubt Anthony, and our family. I was starting to doubt his love for me, especially after hearing that detective slip out the information about Lisa coming to his office.

At the time, I felt that if she came to the office and he didn't tell me, what else was he holding out on. Michael reassured me that

146

everything was going to be okay. He also found her a new residence! I was going to wait and share that info with Anthony after Thanksgiving. Right now, I just wanted to enjoy my man.

Wearing only my panties, I took a couple of breaths and watched my husband. He slept so peacefully. He fell asleep with the book that he was reading lying right next to him. The light that illuminated the room was the one from his reading lamp. The expression on his face was peaceful. I wanted to taste his lips so badly, but I was enjoying just watching him.

I got into bed and snuggled up to my husband's warm body. Automatically his arm lifted for me to lay my head on his chest. Rubbing my fingers up and down his pronounced abs muscles, I felt myself becoming wet. A soft moan escaped his throat as he stirred but did not wake up.

Becoming more excited, I continued to rub his chest, as I straddled my husband, I leaned in and kissed first his bottom lip, and then the top. Opening his eyes, he smiled as he kissed me back. I kissed him passionately, wanting him so badly. Between kisses, I asked Anthony softly, "Will you please fuck me?"

As if I weighed nothing, my husband quickly flipped me over and positioned me on my hands and knees. His lips were so soft as he kissed the skin on my hips and soft ass. He rubbed my legs as he slowly separated them.

"Baby, I miss you," I informed him, my voice barely a whisper. Cupping my breast, I could feel my back beginning to arch.

"Shhh," he replied back, as I felt moisture escaping the fullness of my mound. My instant wetness excited my husband, as he released another moan. He dipped his fingers inside of me over and over, periodically playing with my clit and then sucking those same fingers.

A Cold Piece

My body was trembling as he finally turned me onto my back and stared deeply into my eyes. He watched me as if he was seeing me for the first time, his eyes filled with passion and love.

"What are you thinking?" I asked him, smiling at him mischievously. Not saying a word, he leaned down and kissed my lips, running his tongue across them. The slight gesture caught me by surprise and a warm sensation shot through my body.

Cupping both of her breasts with his hands, he softly pushed them together. He ran each of his index fingers across my tan nipples, making them swell into the shapes of silver dollars.

He placed each of my breasts into his mouth at the same time, teasing my nipples with his tongue. Every nerve in my body was now alert, reminding me of how our sex life was when we first got married. He knew I wanted him to penetrate me, but instead he took his time.

Running soft circles across my stomach and around my belly, a smile crept upon his lips. He enjoyed everything thing that he was doing to me, and the way my body was responding.

I inhaled a deep breath, as I watched him slowly descend down towards my nectar. Tenderly he licked the fullness of my clit, biting and nibbling ever so gently.

Our lovemaking went on into the wee hours of the morning. Each of us took our time exploring each other's bodies, getting acquainted all over again. It has been a long time since we shared an embrace let alone made love.

Peanuts

Daphne

"Yes, Mr. Oliver, the other servants have arrived to assist with the dinner tonight," I informed my boss while slicing up the celery.

"Good job Daphne. I knew you had it all under control. Once I leave here, I am going to head to the airport and pick up Gabrielle's parents. My family will arrive in the morning. Call me if you need me, okay?"

"Yes sir," I replied with a smile. "You know I will."

I sat down on the cordless phone and turned my attention back to the small television set that folded out from the bottom of the kitchen counter. Ms. Gabby got this little contraption for my birthday, and it sure came in handy.

A Wonderful Life was on and since it was Thanksgiving, all of my favorite holiday shows were going to be playing.

"Ms. Daphne, do you need any help with the stuffing?" a small voice interrupted my thoughts. I turned my attention to the small dark-haired woman that stood in the doorway.

"I have finished setting up the tables in the dining area and the parlor, and I didn't want to get into anyone else's way." The young woman held her head down, waiting for me to respond.

There is something familiar about this lady, I thought to myself feeling a slight shiver run through my body. I placed the knife down and rubbed both of my arms.

Shaking off any ill thoughts, I plastered a fake smile onto my face, and waved towards the refrigerator.

Sure, you can help in the kitchen. There are several bowls wrapped in saran wrap. Get them out and help me start chopping the vegetables up. What's your name again sweetie?" I asked, looking her directly into the eyes. "You see, my salt and pepper hair is not just for decoration, it is to remind me of my old age."

We both let out a strained chuckle, and I waited for her to respond.

"My name is Tilly," the young lady told me, opening the door to the fridge. One by one, she removed the bowels and placed them onto the counter.

"Ms. Daphne, do you happen to have any chestnuts?" Tilly asked, turning her attention back to me. "My grandmother taught me this great recipe for stuffing that includes a couple of chopped chests—"

"No, no, no!" I declared slamming the refrigerator door. Mrs. Oliver has a terrible allergy to nuts. Chestnuts, Pecans, Peanuts... She is allergic to the entire family!"

"I, I am sorry," Tilly said, "I didn't know."

A shrill cry rang out, and I removed the baby monitor from my apron.

"Goodness, the baby is awake," I said aloud to no one in particular.

"Um, Tilly, correct?" I asked wiping my hands onto my apron. Just go ahead and chop up the vegetables and stir them into the mixture. That is how you can help me.

I hurried up the stairs to get the baby. He was more like a big boy, and he was growing so well. The Oliver's were blessed when they gave birth to such a well temperament little boy. I hurried and changed his diaper, then asked James, his butler, to set up his swing inside the kitchen so that he could be closer to me.

"Dear Lord,

Thank you for this wonderful meal, that we are about to receive. Thank you to all of the family and friends from near and far that joins us in this room. Also, Lord, bless all of the sick and shut in and make sure that their Thanksgiving is just as beautiful as ours.

Amen."

Everyone said Amen in unison and congratulated Justice, Ms. Loretta's daughter, for saying such a wonderful prayer. We were all gathered around the dining room as one big family, servants and guest. I waited for everyone to take their seats and began instructing the temps to step in and start serving the guest. I looked around for Tilly, but I didn't see her anywhere.

She must be in the kitchen, I thought to myself. I didn't get a chance to thank her for all of her assistance this morning. Once AJ was in full swing, everything else went in a blur.

I excused myself and nodded to the help to follow me into the kitchen. We needed to fill the second round of trays and get ready to serve round two. I barely had the stuffing out of the oven when I heard Mr. Oliver yell his wife's name, and for James to dial 9-1-1.

I rushed back into the dining room, to a dreaded sight. Mrs. Oliver was gasping for air, holding her throat. Everyone was trying to help her, but Mr. Malcolm ordered all of them to take a step back.

"Get my bag out of the car Tracy!" he ordered his wife. "I need an epee pin; I think she is having an allergic reaction.

Thank God Mr. Oliver's brother was a doctor. I stood in shock silently praying that God had his arms wrapped around her.

The sound of sirens could be heard from far away, as Gabrielle fought to maintain consciousness. She continued to gasp for air, holding onto the crevasses of her throat.

Moments later, his wife returned with his bag. He removed a small tool, and quickly stabbed her in the neck. It wasn't until I seen her gasp for a couple of breaths that she inhaled that I was able to make myself come closer.

Tears were running down my face as I bent down and rubbed her hair. "It is going to be okay; I promise you it will," I whispered.

"What is she allergic too?" Malcolm asked his brother. Mr. Oliver, still on his knees, was sobbing uncontrollably. I knew what was going through his mind, so I answered him.

"She is allergic to nuts, but, but I know that I – "I stopped mid sentence and struggled to get up.

Now I remembered why that Tilly girl looked familiar to me. She was the lady from the picture the police showed us the day before the alarm system was installed.

"What is she allergic too so I can tell the EMT workers," Malcolm persisted staring at me.

"She is allergic to nuts," Ms. Loretta said aloud.

"Daphne," Mr. Oliver said shaking his head in disbelief. Tell me that you did not use any nuts while preparing dinner. You know that she can't have that."

All eyes were on me waiting for me to respond.

"No Mr. Oliver," I said staring him square in the eyes. I did not give her any nuts, but I DO know who did."

James already had the door open for the Emergency Response Team. Everyone stepped back to allow them to work on Mrs. Oliver. Malcolm stepped in and filled them in with what was going on.

Mr. Oliver stood up from the floor and nodded for me to go into the kitchen. The hired help was all standing around not knowing what to do.

"You can all go!" he barked out holding the door open for me.

Before he could ask me anything I told him everything that took place this morning. I told him how I specifically told the young lady that Mrs. Oliver was allergic to all nuts. I also told him how I only left her for a moment when I went upstairs to get the baby.

"You know Mr. Oliver, I would NEVER, NEVER do anything to hurt any of you. I consider you my family," I sobbed.

159

Mr. Oliver reached out and I met him, arms wide open.

"I know Daphne, I know," he told me patting my back trying to soothe me. "She was in here, right?" he asked. "So, she should come up on the security cameras. She is just adding more evidence to the case that we already have against her. It is not your fault, remember that."

We stood there for a few more moments before we finally separated. I went over to the sink and was wiping my eyes when the kitchen door was opened again. This time it was Ms. Loretta and Malcolm.

"It was her again, wasn't it," Loretta asked.

Silently, Mr. Oliver nodded his head, confirming their assumptions.

Back Down Memory

Lane

Lisa

Sitting inside the diner where I worked during the day is where I met Darrin. When he showed interest in me, I thought I hit the gold mine. Darrin was in the NFL, and his body was solid as a rock. I knew from that first day that he slid me a hundred-dollar tip, that I wanted to taste him, and by the third day that he came in I had my chance.

It was the off season, and he was in Massachusetts visiting some friends and family. Every day at 3:30 pm, Darrin came in and ordered a slice of apple pie. He would take his time and eat the slice watching my every move.

His intense stare made me uncomfortable but intrigued me at the same time. He only spoke to me one time, and that was to introduce himself. He told me his name and asked me for mine. I told him that I didn't give information to men that I didn't know.

"Well get to know me," he said laughing out loud. He reached out and touched my hand, and that is all she wrote. I fell for him and began sleeping with him on my lunch breaks.

I have heard the many stories of women that were swept off their feet by a famous football or basketball player. I watched Basketball Wives and believed that Darrin was my ticket to the other side.

A Cold Piece

Darrin promised to take me on the road with him. We spoke on the phone all the time, had sexting down to science. That is why when I found out that I was pregnant, I knew that Darrin was going to be happy as I was.

Well, I thought wrong. Once I told him that I was pregnant, he stopped calling, emailing and texting. The last message that he sent me told me that he was engaged to his high school sweetheart and that they already had two kids.

I was so devastated when he stopped communicating with me; I guess those stories were right. I was getting tired of men picking me up and then quickly dropping me back to the floor.

If my baby wasn't going to have a father, neither were his other two children. You can take that to the bank!

I was lying in the bathtub taking a trip down memory lane. I was trying to decipher how the hell I got here. I wanted Monica to stay away, but every man in my life made Monica come back out.

I once read in a book, *The Ultimate No No*, about a group of friends that set up a man, to give him a piece of his own medicine. Their plan blew up in their faces because they allowed one of the friends to date the guy for too long.

I decided to do the same thing, but only use my girlfriend Theresa in my plan. The big difference between my plan and the one in the book is that I was not going to let them fall in love. Hell, they were only going to see each other one time! That is all I needed to get my plan together.

I knew he was going to be in town for his friend Cameron's birthday. I knew where Cameron lived, because I met him there a couple of times. We sat down on the street from Cameron's house, and waited for the crew to leave.

A Cold Piece

We followed them to the night club where they met up with a bunch of guys and some stank ass hoes. We sat for a couple of hours and watched them party in the VIP section. Once I felt that Darrin was drunk enough, I went over to the bar and bought Theresa a drink and dropped an ecstasy pill into her glass. I watched the drink bubble as the pill dissolved in the glass.

I gave her the glass and told her to take a couple of sips. I watched Theresa's body language before I sent her over to the table. I needed her to be feeling good, if she was going to make my plan work.

I watched her saunter over to the VIP section and motion in Darrin's direction. I watched him walk over to her, and laugh at whatever nonsense she was feeding him. It didn't take her long to convince him to let her in to party with them. He poured her a drink and she gulped it down.

"Good job T, Good job," I said under my breath.

She was up there touching herself, and whispering in his ear. I knew that he was going to fall for the bait, and when he did, I was going to be there to clean up the mess.

About an hour later, she convinced him to leave the club with her. I watched as he wrapped her arms around his neck and then guide her down the stairs. I rushed out to Theresa's Expedition and hurried inside the back door that was already unlocked.

I positioned myself on the ground in the third row, and laid there as quietly as I could. My adrenaline was pumping as I waited for them to find her car. I knew that he was not driving, so he had to take her car.

I slightly jumped when I heard the panic button go on and off as Darrin tried to locate the vehicle. Once he realized where the sound was coming from, it didn't take that much longer before I heard the doors unlock and begin to open.

It took him a long time to get her into the car, and then climb into the driver's seat. She giggled uncontrollably at nothing as he started the truck.

"Where do you live," Darrin asked, but that was not a good idea. She was so far gone, that I don't think that she could remember her name, let alone where she lived.

She continued to laugh at nothing, as he pulled out of the parking space.

"Don't worry ma, I know exactly where to take you." He turned up the music and sped down the street. Occasionally I peeked out the window trying to see where exactly he was taking us.

The drive must have gotten to her, because Theresa was asleep and I was glad. Her laugh was getting on my nerves, and I didn't need any witnesses to what I was about to do.

The diner where I worked was about ten minutes away, and that is exactly where he took her. How *ironic*. He pulled to the back of the place like he usually did when were sexing before he dumped me like day old trash.

Darrin turned off the ignition and tapped her to wake up. "Come on baby," he coaxed trying to make her wake up. "Show me everything that you told me that you were going to do to me."

Not looking around, Theresa woke up and started laughing like she never fell asleep. Darrin was already positioned in the middle row unbuttoning his shirt. It took Theresa a moment to comprehend, but she drunkenly climbed over the seats.

They both cooed and moaned as he unzipped his pants and pulled his Johnson out. The moment I heard her gurgling, was when I quietly crawled out of my hiding spot. My heart was pumping so fast, as I stood up over them.

It took Darrin a moment to open his eyes and see that I was behind him, but I didn't give him a chance to speak. I immediately stabbed him in the neck over and over and over again.

Theresa began screaming once she realized that that was his blood landing on her.

"What the hell are you doing?!?" Theresa yelled, suddenly sobering up. "This was not part of the plan!"

"Neither was you sucking his dick either bitch!" I screamed as I stabbed her in the stomach. I turned the knife to the left, and pushed her onto the ground.

"UGH!" I screamed. I am tired of reliving this shit! I want these nightmares to go away! I hated my life, and the things that I do. I don't know why these men make me do this shit to them.

I have lost everything, including Anthony. All I want is a baby! Is that so much to ask for? First Darrin didn't want our child and then Anthony took my baby from me through a broken promise. He gave that bitch a baby so fast, but would cum in a towel when it came to me. He was going to give me my baby one way or another!

The police were looking for me, and I definitely could not go back to Minnesota. I feel like I am at the end of my rope and there is no place left to go but up. Believe me; no one is going to stop me from achieving my goals.

Enough is Enough

Loretta

"Meet me at the Chili's by your house in 45 minutes," was all that Gabrielle said to me before the phone went dead. I tried to call her back, but she would not answer. Both sets of twins were hanging out with friends and I was excited! Every time I had an opportunity to rest, it was interrupted by some emergency, so I don't know why I thought this time was going to be different.

Fifteen minutes later, I rolled out of my bed, and pulled on a pair of sweats. I tried to call Gabrielle again, but still no response.

I wonder what this chick got up her sleeve, I thought to myself. I was with her when she met up with Michael, the private investigator, but since her allergic reaction, she hasn't talked about it.

I knew that she confessed to Anthony about meeting up with Michael, after they watched their home surveillance videos and it was confirmed that Lisa was the one who tried to kill her yet again.

Lisa was left alone only for a couple of minutes but that is all that she needed. According to the video, she had a sandwich bag filled with finely chopped chestnuts hidden in her pocket. Once she was by herself, she poured the nuts into the stuffing mix.

Gabrielle recited all the information that Michael told her about Lisa's past life as Monica. Most of the news that she gave him, Anthony already knew except.... The waiter that recognized Lisa, and made her perfect life crumble right before her eyes was now dead. He moved to Baltimore to attend the University of Maryland @ Baltimore and was working at the restaurant part time. He was only on the east coast for nine weeks before his roommate found him floating in their bathtub. His death was almost identical to Mother Elizabeth's and there was only a three day window between the two.

If we were not convinced that this bitch was after Gabrielle, it was very obvious now. Now the only answers we needed were: where is Lisa getting all her information from? How did she know we were in Los Angeles? How did she know what Mo was driving? How did she know what Gabrielle was allergic too? Trying to figure out this woman made me so uncomfortable, and chills ran up and down my spine.

I parked my car and searched the lot for Gabby's. I didn't see it, so I tried to call her again. Oh no, again no response. Sighing, I got out of my vehicle, and went inside. I only waited for a moment before the happy waitress appeared asking me how many was in my party.

I informed her just two and was quickly seated. I had just ordered a Long Island when Gabrielle popped up at the table.

"Make that two please?" she asked the waitress hanging her purse on the back of the chair. I stood up and hugged my friend closely. I tried to read her expression, but it was blank and cold.

Once we were seated I continued to study her body language. Appearing okay, I sipped on my complimentary water and finally asked, "What is going on?"

"I know where she is Lo. I know where that conniving bitch is at right now." The look on Gabrielle's face was so solemn as she spoke. "Michael located her. Here, I am about to text you her address."

"Ooo Kay," slowly I replied. Her tone was making me nervous, but I did want to know where exactly she was going with this. "So that is good news right? Did you let the Detective know? When are they going to arrest her?"

I flashed a weak smile and waited for her response. By the look on her face, I know that whatever she was planning had nothing to do with the police.

"I need you to go with me. I am not calling the police. She always seems to get away. They are *still* looking for her now for questioning, and we gave them the *FUCKING* tape of her in my damn house!" Gabby exclaimed, slamming her hand on the table.

The other patrons in the restaurant were starting to look in our direction; the waitress came over to make sure that everything was okay.

I quickly reassured her that we were fine, and to give us a couple more moments for us to order.

"Gabrielle, I love you baby, you know I do, but... I am not going with you anywhere. We both have children to live for. I mean, you are going to go over there right, and then what? You have not thought this shit out completely. You couldn't have."

I folded my arms across my chest, and reclined back in the chair. I knew that this shit was nerve wracking, but I think she is starting to go crazy. That bitch has basically taken all of us on, and has been winning. I was not trying to take her on head on.

"Lo, you don't have to understand where I am coming from, and I respect your decision, but I need to do this to get my life and sanity back. I am letting her win by not doing anything. It has been a week since she tried to kill me in my own home in front of all my love ones. I can't keep living in fear."

Gabby continued, "She killed Ant's mom! She killed Mo and almost burnt Dricie to death. Tried to kill me, on at least three occasions that I know of. She put her hands on AJ, on my only son; that bitch ain't getting away with it. Lo, this is something that I have to do girl... With or without you."

Gabrielle stood up and dropped two twenties on the table. "I love you Lo, but enough is enough!"

She kissed me on the head, gathered her belongings, downed the rest of the Long Island and left me at the table all alone with my thoughts.

My cell phone vibrated on the table, and I picked it up. I checked my text message screen. There were two messages from Gabrielle. The first had the address and the second one read:

I Love You. If something happens to me, please take care of AJ, the same way you take care of the girls.

From the Pen of *Nicola*

A Cold Piece

Anthony

It has been a long day at the office, and I was so ready to get home. I have been in and out of meetings all day, that I was just ready to go home and cuddle up in the bed with my mamacita. As I quickly gathered my things preparing to depart, I closed my briefcase and I grabbed my cell. *Damn,* I said to myself. I have been going so hard today that I didn't even realize that my cell phone was dead until just now.

"Oh well, I will put it on the charger once I get in the car." saying out loud to no one in particular. Taking in a deep breath, I gladly headed out the door and hurried to the elevator.

The building was silent as usual, but tonight felt different. I felt a lump in my throat and a knot in my stomach, but I didn't know where the feeling was coming from. I tried to shake it off, but it wouldn't go away. I unlocked the door to my Range Rover, and waited a minute before I actually entered.

I turned on the ignition, plugged the charger into the igniter, and hooked up my Black Berry. I shifted my truck into drive, and pulled out of the parking garage.

Once I was out on the main road, I turned on my cell phone. It didn't take long for the alerts on my phone to start going off.

Stopping at the red light is when I actually checked the notification history. There were several messages, but only two that I cared about. One from Gabrielle that simply read:

A Cold Piece

I Love You.

And the other was from Loretta. Her message scared the hell out of me, and I immediately forwarded it to Detective Harris. The message read:

Anthony, was just w Gabby. She is tryin 2 meet up w Lisa. I'm goin 2 send u address. Tried 2 call u couple of times. Will keep calling.

My heart was in my throat as I called the detective.

"Just finished reading your message, I was just about to call you," Detective Harris said answering the phone. "I am going to call in for back up, and I'm on my way there now. Where are you?" she asked waiting for me to respond.

"I am leaving my office downtown, about ten minutes away from West Oak Street. I haven't done anything to save my family, but I swear on my son's life, I am going to save my wife!"

I dropped the phone on the passenger seat, and opened my glove compartment. Inside was the nine millimeter gun that I purchased the day after that bitch blew up my wife's car. Driving fast and erratically, I hurried to get to the address that Lo sent me.

Once I turned onto Oak Street, it did not take me long to spot my wife's car. I picked up my phone and called her phone. It didn't ring at all, just went straight to voicemail.

Saying a silent prayer to the Lord to take care of my wife, I took a couple of deep breaths and got out of my truck. I stuck the gun inside the back of my pants and hurried to the door.

I didn't know exactly what I was going to do, but I knew I needed to hurry. The sound of my heart was echoing in my ears as I got closer to the door. Seeing that it was ajar, I decided to go inside and investigate the scene.

I pushed open the door just enough for me to go in. The house was eerily silent. I tried to adjust my eyes to the darkness as I continued my trek inside. The scent of death that resonated throughout the house was horrifying. Spotting the staircase, I decided to go upstairs. Right before I could take a step, I heard the front door slam shut, causing me to nearly jump damn near out of my skin.

"I knew that you would be her knight in shining armor. The same hero that you promised me to be," Lisa said standing in front of the door.

I couldn't believe that this was the same woman that I said I DO too. She appeared to have aged tremendously. Her eyes appeared as if they were sunken into her head and her precious hair was limp. She held a gun with her right hand, and locked the door know with her left.

"Where's Gabrielle," I asked in a calm tone.

Lisa cocked her head over to the left, and flashed me a crooked smile.

"Oh, are you talking about the bitch that you allowed to carry your seed, but made me kill mine? She is upstairs. You know, you think you are pretty slick don't you?" Lisa asked me still pointing the gun at me.

"First sending that package to me unsigned after the birth of your damn son. Do you think 50,000 dollars is enough to get rid of me? Anthony are you listening to me? I never wanted your fucking money. I wanted your punk ass to love me and give me a child. That's it! Nothing else!"

"Nothing Else! Nothing Else!" I screamed. "Bitch you lied to me, telling me your name was fucking Lisa and your name really was Monica, wanted in connection in the murder of your ex-boyfriend."

I tried to continue, but she held up her finger to her lips.

"Shhhh. I am not done. I will give you an opportunity to talk; it's more courtesy than you have ever given me. I begged you to talk to me. Tell me why you ended our marriage so abruptly. You just left me out to dry like a piece of laundry. You wouldn't give me the answers that I wanted, soooo, I went and paid your precious mother a visit."

Tears swelled in my eyes, as she confirmed my biggest fear. I listen to her tell me how she murdered my mother by putting something in her drink, making it look like she died in the tub, but not until she gave her some key information.

"She told me all about Michael, and how he did the background investigation on me. Well, I met up with Michael, and gave him a piece of this pretty pussy that you threw out to dry. After that, he was puddy in my hands, telling me EVERYTHING about you and your damn family.

What investigator *follows* *up* with their clients to get status checks? I told you baby that you were too trusting and a creature of habit. Those two things together allowed me to put together this beautiful plan. You want to see your bitch. Go ahead. Take your ass up those stairs and find her."

I was frozen in my spot, unable to move. My thoughts were running wild, taking in everything that she was telling me. It was all making sense now. Michael was feeding her our information, and like a dummy, I was giving it to him.

She just confessed to killing my mother to my face. Tears flowed down my face as I tried to either move or speak. I felt as if I was in a horrific dream and was waiting for someone to wake me and remove me from this nightmare.

Lisa came up behind me and pushed me forward with the barrel of her gun.

"GO UPSTAIRS NOW!" she yelled while pushing me again. Shaking out of it, I headed up the stairs scared to death. Gabrielle was right. She was going to stop at nothing to kill her.

I began to speak saying, "So you knew why I left, and it had nothing to do with Gabby or her friends, but you continued to ask why I left... you a sick bitch."

"Shut the fuck up," she said as she pushed the barrel of the gun in my back. She continued as we went up the stairs, "You promised me that we would be together and you up and leave, then you start a happy life with that Latina bitch.

The stairs creaked as we neared the top. The house was old and spider webs were everywhere. When we reached the top, Lisa directed me to go to the room on the left.

I opened the door, not knowing what to expect. The entire time that I was inside I hadn't heard a peep from my wife, which was making me think that she was already dead.

"Come on out baby, his foolish ass came alone." Lisa said out loud.

The closet door slowly opened and out came Michael clutching my wife close to him, covering her mouth. Both of them were breathing heavily, and Gabrielle was crying.

I pulled the gun out from my waist and pointed it at his head.

"Let my wife go Michael. This has nothing to do with you." I informed him cocking my gun into ready position."

A Cold Piece

"Put that thing down baby. You don't know how to use it." Lisa damn near dropped her gun laughing at me.

I took her laughter as my opportunity to show everyone in the room that I was not a joke and shot three rounds, two into Michael's head and one into his neck.

Blood shot out everywhere, hitting Gabrielle directly in the face. Michael collapsed taking my wife with him.

Screaming, Lisa let out five rounds from her gun. Dropping my gun, I ran trying to dodge her bullets getting closer to the window. She fired another shot, this time hitting me on the arm and sending me out of the window.

Falling through the big oak tree located outside of the window, it felt like an eternity for me to have impact with the ground. Once I landed, I waited a moment before I tried to stand up. I felt so weak and broken but I had to save my wife from that crazy woman.

I hopped to the front door and tried to get it open. "Gabrielle!" I screamed kicking the door. I could hear her screaming for her life from inside, and there was nothing that I could do about it. My left arm was limp and bloody and could still see the smoke coming from the hole that the bullet created.

I prayed under my breath,

"Dear Lord, please help her. Please let me save her," as I continued to kick the door.

Lisa was at the end of her rope, and there was no point of return. She believed that her life was over, and there was only one person to blame, and that was Gabrielle.

My body was weak, my vision was getting blurry, but I could not give up. My Gabby was in danger, and I was the cause. That was the worse feeling in the world.

Another gunshot blast rung out; Gabrielle yelled out again.

Where the hell is the police, I thought to myself, feeling helpless and insecure. Taking in a deep breath, I attempted to regain my composure as I kicked the door hopefully for the last time.

Boom! Another gunshot rang out. This time it was not followed by a cry, but silence, damn what a cold piece.

Epilogue

Gabrielle

Shaking, I went over to Lisa's crumpled body lying on the floor. I kicked her twice to see if she would move. Not trusting this bitch, I used the butt of the gun and hit her over and over on her head. Each time I connected, the fear that had been harboring inside of me because of her, felt as if it was being lifted from my body. I hit her for my son who she tried to make motherless. I hit her for Monique who she killed trying to kill me. I hit her for Andrice who she burnt trying to blow me up. Finally, with the last blow and all my anger and hate in my heart and arms, I hit her for me.

I got up and hurried down the steps. I could hear the sirens coming closer. I had to let my husband know that I was okay. When Michael called me this morning and told me that he would go with me to see Lisa, I was delighted. Part of me was afraid, but the other part of me wanted to meet this fear head on and fight it.

It wasn't until inside that I learned that the pair was working together. Lisa was telling me why she hated me when we heard Anthony pull up. She told Michael to hide from me, which is how we ended up in the closet.

The moment Anthony went out the window was when I knew that this was it. Lisa turned her attention to me and fired the first shot. Jumping out of the way, I scrambled trying to get Anthony's gun off the splintered floor. She shot at me a second time, hoping to connect. Picking up his gun, shakily I pointed the barrel at her. She laughed at me like she did Anthony, underestimating what I would do. Pulling that hammer back, just like a marksman, that one shot I fired connected with her chest and I watched her drop to the floor.

Struggling to get the front door open, I needed to escape this nightmare. My hands shook trying to work the unlock button. I flung the door open to be greeted by the evening air and my love.

Collapsed by the front door in a pool of his own blood, was my Anthony shaking and crying but alive. I was ashamed that I ever doubted the love that he had for me. I was ashamed that I doubted the bond that we shared.

Bending down, I tried to calm him down.

"Baby, it's over," I whispered to him. He looked up staring at me in disbelief.

"Gabby. Gabrielle. Is that you?" he asked quietly. "I thought that you were d—"."

"Shhh my love. No, I am fine. Like I said, it's over."

Struggling to get him up, Detective Harris ran up to help me.

"Where is she?" she asked. "Are you okay?"

Confirming that I was alright, but Anthony had been wounded, I pointed upstairs. Detective Harris helped me guide Anthony to the ambulance and signaled for the officers to go inside and upstairs to see what had been done by that 9mm cold piece of steel.

Reviews

If you enjoy this story, please leave a review.
This is how others will know to take the time
and read a novel from the pen of Ni'cola!
Thank you so much!

Just click on the following link:

http://amzn.to/Hg5IoL

Introducing

Ni'cola Mitchell

Striving to inject her unique flair into the realm of contemporary fiction, Award-Winning, Best-Selling author Ni'cola Mitchell entered the literary scene with one main objective: To Stimulate Your Mind, One Word at a Time.

Through her independent publishing company NCM Publishing, Ni'cola published numerous titles which have been featured on various best-selling lists throughout the country. Much of her work revolves around complex relationship issues and Mitchell's compulsive desire to see women overcome challenges.

Over and Over Again was featured in the top ten by EDC Creations Recommended Reading List for the 2009 fall season under Mainstream Fiction and Women's Fiction. Ni'cola Mitchell was nominated Self-Published Author of the Year with the African American Literary Award Show for 2010 and 2011. Her short story "The Forbidden Rain" was featured in the Between the Sheets anthology which won 2011 Anthology of the Year with the African

American Literary Award Show. Recently Twisted, won Book of the Year for 2011 with the African American on the Move Book Club.

Because of her outstanding representation of Las Vegas' African American community, Ni'cola Mitchell was featured in the second edition of Who's Who in Black Las Vegas. Ni'cola was also included in the fourth volume of the I Am Royalty: Profiles in Black History series. She is also a motivational speaker and literary consultant. When she isn't writing, Mitchell loves to spend time with her family and volunteer as a mentor for youth activities.

Currently, Ni'cola Mitchell is touring across the country, speaking about the importance of going after your dreams and overcoming obstacles, and how to self-publish your book successfully. Originally from Kingston, Jamaica, Mitchell currently resides in North Las Vegas, Nevada, with her two daughters, Destani, and Diamond. Co-Founder of the Baltimore Urban Book Festival, Ni'cola holds a bachelor's degree of Science in Business Management and is currently pursuing a Master of Business Administration in Small Business. To find out more check out www.nicolacmitchell.com.

OBSESSIVE SOUL MEDIA PRESENTS

HE'S MY FAVORITE
Mistake

from the pen of
NI'COLA & TAMIKA

Printed in Great Britain
by Amazon